"If we're not enemies, what exactly are we?"

"That's a good question." Which wasn't an answer at all.

The elevator doors slid open and Cooper stepped outside. He stopped, looked at her and then held out his hand to her again. Silently, he waited, and Terri's mind raced.

She could refuse. Go back down to her suite and never know why he'd wanted to take her to the roof. She could turn away from this opportunity to talk to him, away from everyone else, to maybe find common ground that could help them both.

Or she could fight her fear of heights and go with him.

Not a hard decision at all, because she'd never been one to back away from what scared her. But that wasn't all of it, either. He was so gorgeous, so intense, and when he looked at her, Terri felt heat simmer inside her bones.

Dear Reader,

I love Las Vegas. There. I admitted it. Yes, I love the neon, the casinos, the gorgeous hotels and the hot desert wind that seems to always be sweeping across the city. During the day, Vegas can be bland, almost like any other city in the world.

But at night, Las Vegas shines. It bursts into electric life and shatters every shadow in brilliant light and color.

So it was fun to set this book in one of my favorite places. *Tempt Me in Vegas* is a fun, sexy story about what can happen when wishes come true.

Cooper Hayes is owner and CEO of a chain of luxury hotels all over the world. When his partner dies, he expects to be solely in charge. That's when he finds out his partner had a daughter that no one—including the daughter—knew about.

Terri Ferguson was adopted at birth and knew nothing about the biological parents she never met. Then her birth father dies and names her as his heir. Suddenly, Terri's everyday, ordinary life in Ogden, Utah, is changed forever.

When Cooper and Terri meet in Vegas, these two wildly different people clash almost instantly. Cooper wants to buy her out, but Terri's not going anywhere.

I really hope you enjoy this book as much as I did writing it! Please stop by Facebook to say hello, and if you love this book, I'd love for you to review it on Goodreads or Amazon!

Happy reading!

Until next time,

Maureen Child

MAUREEN CHILD

TEMPT ME IN VEGAS

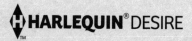

Recycling programs
for this product may
not exist in your area.

ISBN-13: 978-1-335-97179-1

Tempt Me in Vegas

Copyright © 2018 by Maureen Child

Printed in U.S.A.

Maureen Child writes for the Harlequin Desire line and can't imagine a better job. A seven-time finalist for a prestigious Romance Writers of America RITA® Award, Maureen is the author of more than one hundred romance novels. Her books regularly appear on bestseller lists and have won several awards, including a Prism Award, a National Readers' Choice Award, a Colorado Romance Writers Award of Excellence and a Golden Quill Award. She is a native Californian but has recently moved to the mountains of Utah.

Books by Maureen Child

Harlequin Desire

The Baby Inheritance
Maid Under the Mistletoe
The Tycoon's Secret Child
A Texas-Sized Secret
Little Secrets: His Unexpected Heir
Rich Rancher's Redemption
Billionaire's Bargain
Tempt Me in Vegas

Texas Cattleman's Club: Bachelor Auction

Runaway Temptation

Visit her Author Profile page at Harlequin.com, or maureenchild.com, for more titles.

One

"This isn't a damn soap opera. It's real life." Cooper Hayes jammed both hands into his slacks pockets and shot a glare at the man opposite him. "How the hell did this happen? Secret heirs don't just appear at the reading of a damn will."

"The only thing that *appeared* was her name," Dave Carey reminded him.

True, but hardly consolation. Cooper stared at the other man for a few long beats. Dave had been his best friend and confidant since college. He was always reasonable, logical and so damn cool-headed that it was irritating at times. Like now, for instance.

"That's enough, though, isn't it? *She* exists. She has a name. And now," Cooper added darkly, "apparently, *half* of my company. To top it all off, we know nothing about her."

Here in his office on the twentieth floor of the StarFire Hotel, Cooper could let his frustration show. In front of the board and the company's fleet of lawyers, he'd had to hide his surprise and his anger at the reading of Jacob Evans's will.

Usually, being in this room with its wide windows, plush carpeting and luxurious furnishings helped to center Cooper. To remind him how far the company had come under his direction. As did looking at the paintings of the famed Hayes hotels that decorated the walls. His father and Jacob had started the company, but it was Cooper who had built it into the huge success it was today.

But at the moment it was hard to take comfort in his business…his world, when the very foundations had been shaken.

Cooper still couldn't quite wrap his head around any of this. Hell, he'd had everything planned out most of his life. Hayes Corporation had been his birthright. He'd trained for years to take the helm of the company and he'd damn near single-handedly made his hotels synonymous with *luxury*.

Though there were five star Hayes hotels all around the world, their main headquarters was here, in what was considered the flagship hotel, the StarFire, in Las Vegas. The building had undergone massive renovations over the years, but it still claimed a huge swath of the famed Vegas Strip, and at night it glowed as fiercely as the stars it had been named after.

When Trevor died, Cooper had stepped into his father's place and worked with Jacob. Since the man had no family, it was understood that when Jacob died, the company would fall completely to Cooper, who had been raised to be king.

Except it hadn't worked out that way.

Cooper looked at Dave again. Now his executive assistant, he and Dave had both worked summers for the corporation, interned in different departments to learn as much as they could and, when Cooper took over from his father, Dave had come along with Cooper. He couldn't really imagine doing this job without Dave. Having someone you could trust was priceless.

Dave sat in one of the maroon leather guest chairs opposite Cooper's massive mahogany desk. He wore a black suit with a red power tie. His brown hair was cut short and his dark brown eyes were thoughtful. "We don't know much *now*. We will, though, in a couple of hours. I've got our best men working on it."

"Fine," Cooper muttered darkly as impatience clawed at his insides. "Jacob had a daughter. A daughter no one knew about. Still sounds like a bad plot in a B movie." Unbelievable. Apparently, Jacob *did* have family after all. A daughter he'd never seen. One he and the child's mother had given up for adoption nearly thirty years ago. And he had waited until he was *dead* to make the damn announcement.

Pushing one hand through his black hair, Cooper shook his head. "You'd think Jacob could have given me a heads-up about this."

"Maybe he planned to," Dave offered, then shut up fast when Cooper glared at him.

"I've known him my whole damn life," he reminded his friend. "Jacob couldn't find five minutes in the last thirty-five years to say, 'Oh, did I tell you I have a daughter?'"

"If you're waiting for me to explain this away," Dave said, lifting both hands in an elegant shrug, "you've got a long wait. I can't tell you why he never told you. I can say that Jacob probably wasn't expecting to die in a damn golf-cart accident."

True. If that cart hadn't rolled, Jacob wouldn't have broken his damn neck and—*it wouldn't have changed anything.* Jacob had been eighty years old. This would all have happened, eventually.

"He gave her up for adoption, ignored her existence for years, then leaves her his half of the company?" Cooper took a deep breath, hoping for calm that didn't come. "Who does that?"

Dave didn't answer because there was no answer. At this point all Cooper had were questions. Who was this woman? What would she say when she found out she was a damn heiress? Would she expect to have a say in how Cooper's business was run? That stopped him cold. No way was she going to interfere in the company; he didn't care who the hell she was.

"Okay," he said, nodding to himself as his thoughts coalesced. "I want to know everything there is to know about—" he broke off and looked down at the copy of Jacob's will laying on his desk "—Terri Ferguson, by the end of today. Where she went to school, what she does, who she knows. Hell, I want to know what she eats for breakfast.

"If I'm going to have to deal with her, I want to have as much ammunition going into this fight as I possibly can."

"Got it." Dave stood up and turned for the door. "Maybe we'll get lucky. Maybe she won't want any of this."

Cooper would have laughed, but he was too furious. "Sure, that'll happen. People turn down billions of dollars every day."

Nodding, Dave said, "Right."

"No, she won't turn it down," Cooper was saying, more to himself than to his friend. "But she's not going to show up out of nowhere and be a part of the company. I don't care who she is. Maybe what we have to do here is find a way to convince her to take the money and then disappear."

"Worth a shot," Dave said. "I'll push our guys to research faster."

"Good."

Once his friend was gone, Cooper turned toward the wall of windows at his back. He stared down at Las Vegas Boulevard, better known as the bustling Vegas Strip, nearly thirty floors below, and let his thoughts wander. He'd grown up in this hotel and still lived in one of the owner's suites on the twenty-fifth floor. He knew every nook and cranny of this city and loved every mercenary inch of it.

On the street, tourists wandered with hope in their hearts and cash in their wallets. They played the machines, the gaming tables and in the bingo parlors. Every last one of them had thoughts of going home rich.

Why would Jacob's long-lost daughter be any different?

His gaze swept the hotels that surrounded his own and he noticed, not for the first time, that in daylight Vegas held little of the magic that shone on it at night. The city slept during the day but with darkness, it burst into exuberant life.

Cooper's family had been part of Vegas history for decades, he reminded himself as he turned back to his desk. He'd taken his father's legacy and made it a worldwide brand. Cooper had made his mark through hard work, single-minded diligence and a vision of exactly what he wanted.

Damned if he'd let some interloper crash the party.

"I'm sorry." Terri Ferguson shook her head and almost pinched herself, just to make sure she wasn't dreaming. But one look around the employee break room at the bank where she worked convinced her that this was all too real. Just fifteen minutes ago she'd been downstairs on the teller line, helping Mrs. Francis make a deposit. Now she was here, sitting across from a very fussy-looking lawyer listening to what seemed like a fairy tale. Apparently, starring *her*.

"Would you mind saying all of that one more time?"

The lawyer, Maxwell Seaton, sighed. "Ms. Ferguson, I've already explained this twice. How many more times will be required?"

Terri heard the snotty attitude in the older man's tone and maybe there was a part of her that couldn't blame him for it. But come on. Wouldn't anyone in her current position be a little off balance? Because none of this made sense.

It had been an ordinary day in Ogden, Utah. She'd gone to work, laughed with her friends, then taken her spot on the teller line at the Wasatch Bank in downtown Ogden. Familiar customers had streamed in and out of the bank until this man had approached her and, in a few words, turned her whole world upside down.

Now the older man removed his glasses, gave another sigh, then plucked a handkerchief from his suit pocket and unnecessarily cleaned the lenses. "As I've made clear to you, Ms. Ferguson, I represent your biological father's estate."

"My father," she whispered, the very word feeling a little foreign. Terri had grown up knowing she was adopted. Her parents had always told her the truth, that she had been *chosen* by them because they fell in love with her the moment they saw her. They'd encouraged her to search for her birth parents once she was eighteen, but Terri hadn't been curious. Why would she be? she'd reasoned. Where she'd come from didn't really matter as much as where she was, right?

Besides, she hadn't wanted to hurt her mother or father. Then her dad died, her mother moved to southern Utah to live with her sister, and Terri had been too busy with college and life to worry about a biological connection to people she didn't know.

Now that connection had just jumped up to bite her on the butt.

"Yes, your father. Jacob Evans." The lawyer slipped his glasses back into place. "He recently passed away and in accordance with his will, I'm here to inform you that you are his sole beneficiary."

And that summed up the weird. Why would he have left her anything? They had no connection beyond biology. And if he'd known who she was, why hadn't Jacob Evans ever reached out to her? Well, those were questions she would never get an answer to.

"Right. Okay. And I inherited a hotel?" She took a breath and held up one hand before he could speak again. "I'm really sorry. Normally, I'm not this slow on the uptake. Honestly. But this is…just so bizarre."

For the first time since entering the bank and asking to speak to her privately, the lawyer gave her a small smile. "I do understand how unexpected this must seem to you."

"'Unexpected' is a good word," she agreed and reached for the water bottle in front of her. She took a sip and added, "Weird is better."

"I suppose." Another smile. "Ms. Ferguson, your father was a full partner in the Hayes Corporation."

"Okay…" That meant exactly nothing to her.

He sighed. "The Hayes Corporation owns more than two thousand hotels, all over the world."

"Two *thousand*?" She heard her own voice squeak and winced at the sound. But seriously? Two thousand hotels? That couldn't be right, could it? Her stomach did a quick pitch and roll and Terri took a deep breath trying to calm it.

The smell of burning coffee from the pot on the counter flavored the air, and the bank's furnace made a soft hum of background noise. Downstairs people were working, talking, laughing, living normal lives, and up here? Terri was trying to *think*. Tried to remember who she was, where she was. But her brain had apparently decided it had accepted enough information for one day and shut down.

Resting one hand on a sheaf of papers he had stacked on the table, Mr. Seaton looked at her steadily. At least the gleam of impatience was gone from his eyes. Maybe he was finally understanding what a shock all of this was to her.

"Once you sign these papers, it's official," he told her. "You'll have your father's share in a very successful company."

She tipped her head to one side and quietly asked, "*How* successful?"

One corner of his mouth twitched slightly. "*Very*. You, Ms. Ferguson, are now an extremely wealthy woman."

Wealthy. Rich. Also weird. But good. Because her cable bill had just gone up and she had just been forced to put new brakes on her car and with winter coming, she really wanted to get new insulation on her windows and—

She reached for the papers instinctively, then pulled her hand back. "I'd like my own lawyer to look these over before I sign." Well, her late father's lawyer, but that didn't really matter, did it?

"Commendable," he said with a brief nod. Standing, he closed his black leather briefcase with a snap. Looking down at her, he said, "Your new partner, Mr. Cooper Hayes, is at the company headquarters in Las Vegas. He'd like to see you there as soon as possible."

"Cooper Hayes." She should probably write that down.

"Yes. His contact information is included in the packet of papers." He gave her a small smile. "Hayes Corporation is headquartered at the StarFire Hotel and Casino."

StarFire. She'd heard of it, of course. Seen pictures in magazines and now that she thought of it, Terri had seen pictures of Cooper Hayes, too. Her mind drew up one of the images of him posing with some celebrity or other—naturally, he was tall and gorgeous with eyes so blue he had to be wearing colored contacts.

And now he was her *partner.* The idea of going to the StarFire, meeting Cooper Hayes on his home turf, was a little intimidating, but she didn't see a way around it. After all, she was now half owner of the place. A shocked burst of laughter bubbled up in her chest, but she squashed it. Yesterday she wouldn't have been able to afford to *stay* at the StarFire. Now she owned half of it.

Weird just kept getting weirder.

"Okay, thank you." She glanced at the papers, but didn't touch them.

"Ms. Ferguson," the man said quietly, and waited

until her gaze met his to continue. "I know this is all new and somewhat overwhelming—"

"Somewhat?" she laughed but the sound she made sounded a little hysterical so she stopped. Fast.

"But," he continued calmly, "I believe once the surprise of the situation eases, you'll do very well in your new life."

"You think so?"

"I do." He grabbed the doorknob and said, "I've left my card with the papers, as well. If you have any questions or concerns, please feel free to call me."

"Thank you."

He opened the door and Jan Belling almost fell into the room. She recovered quickly, stumbling to catch her balance, then flashing the lawyer a brilliant smile. "Hi, sorry."

"No need," he said, lips twitching. Giving Terri one last nod, he left.

Jan slipped into the room, closed the door and hurried over to take a seat opposite Terri. Her short, spiky black hair complemented bottle-green eyes, making her look like a pixie. "Well," she said, "that was embarrassing."

"I can't believe you were listening at the door."

"I can't believe you're surprised. Besides, I didn't hear much. The door's too thick. Stupid historical buildings with real wood doors." Jan took a breath. "So what happened? Who was he and why did he want you?"

Terri laughed as the tension she'd been feeling for the past fifteen minutes dissipated. Jan was her best friend, and the one person who could help her make sense of all of this. "Speaking of a 'can't believe' situation…"

"Try me."

Terri shook her head at the strangeness of it all. "I want to tell you all of it, but I should get back to work."

Jan shook her head. "No worries. The boss says you can take as long as you like. We're not busy, anyway, so start talking."

Turning her bottle of water back and forth between her hands, Terri did. As she told her friend everything, it all began to settle in her own mind. It was beyond strange. Crazy. Impossible, even. Okay, maybe her mind wasn't as settled as she'd thought.

"This is like a fairy tale or something," Jan finally said once Terri had wound down.

"That's exactly what I was thinking," Terri admitted wryly. "So when the clock strikes midnight do I turn back into a pumpkin?"

"Cinderella wasn't a pumpkin. Her carriage was." Jan laughed a little. "And this is reality no matter how strange it all seems. This is amazing, Terri. You're rich. I mean *wildly* rich."

"Oh, God." Terri dropped one hand to her stomach in a futile attempt to calm it. She'd never had a lot of money. Growing up, her adoptive parents had been schoolteachers, so though they'd had a nice life, they'd also driven ten-year-old cars and saved up to take vacations.

Of course, she drove to Idaho occasionally to buy lottery tickets, because who didn't dream of suddenly becoming a gazillionaire? But to have it actually *happen* was almost terrifying.

Jan reached across the table to take her hand. "Why aren't you celebrating? Oh. Wait. Sorry. God, I'm an idiot sometimes. You're reacting to hearing that your biological father died, aren't you?"

"Seems ridiculous to be sad about someone you've never met, but yeah, I guess I am." In the midst of the windfall, there was that sad fact. Terri silently wondered what her father had been like. If he had known who and where she was, why had he never contacted her before? Why had he left her everything? She'd probably always wonder.

Jan took Terri's water, had a sip, then handed it back. "You really had no idea at all about who your biological father was?"

"Not a clue," she said softly. "And now I've got all these questions and no way to get answers and... I don't know. It's all so far out there, it's hard to believe it's really happening."

"Yeah, I get that. But," Jan said, "at least you know he thought about you. Remembered you. And in the end, wanted to give you everything he had."

A smile tugged at the corner of Terri's mouth. "Good point. Okay, then. No feeling sorry for myself. But I can be a little panicked, right?"

"Absolutely. The StarFire?" Jan grinned. "That's supposed to be an amazing hotel."

"I know." Terri took a deep breath, but she had a feeling the wild tremors inside weren't going to be soothed away. Her entire world had just been rocked.

Terri's mind raced with possibilities. She had a good job, if not an exciting one, but now she had been given the chance for more. Sure, she'd have a lot to learn, but stepping into this new life could be amazing.

"And you *own* it!"

"Well I own half of it, apparently." Abruptly, Terri stood up and said, "How do I go from being a bank teller to being a hotel executive?"

"Seriously?" Jan looked at her. "You're going to make me mad if you start doubting yourself. Okay, fine, there's the whole surprise factor to take into account," Jan said. "But you're smart and you're good with people and you can do any damn thing you want to."

Smiling, Terri said, "Thanks for that."

"You're welcome."

"I don't even know where to start, Jan."

"With a lawyer." Jan stood, too, and her expression read sympathy and aggravation. "Terri, this is your big chance. A chance to get out of the bank, to find a job that really interests you. Take it and run."

All true. Terri had taken this job at the bank because she needed to work. But it wasn't where she'd wanted to build a career. She really hadn't known what she wanted. And the longer she stayed at the bank, the more comfortable it became and the less likely it was that she would leave to find something that fit her better.

She'd always done the expected thing. School. Work. Maybe this was the Universe giving her the opportunity to burst out of her rut and find out just what she was capable of.

Jan was right. She had to take this chance. Had to try for... more.

"Your new partner expects to see you in Vegas and you've got to figure all of this out before you meet him."

Terri blew out a breath. She wasn't a coward. Never had been. Sure, she'd never been faced with anything like this in her life before, but she could do it.

Couldn't she?

She'd always been the good girl. The good daughter. The responsible one. She'd had dreams of traveling but had accepted that for the things she'd wanted to do and see, she would have to spend years saving money. Now suddenly, the world was laid out in front of her. She'd be crazy to ignore it.

"You're right," she said, nodding. "I'll talk to Mike, tell him I need to take some time off."

Jan shook her head and smiled. "While you're talking to the bank manager, you might tell him that you're going to be taking off *forever*."

Terri laughed. "Things are changing, yes. But I'm not ready to throw my whole life out just yet."

"I think," Jan said as they left the break room together, "someone already did that for you."

"I hate it when you're right."

Jan laid a hand on her arm. "Terri, you're making yourself nuts and you don't have to. Cooper Hayes doesn't need you to run the company. But you're his new partner, like it or not, so you do at least get a say in things."

True, she thought and her mind started racing again.

This was the opportunity of a lifetime and she'd be crazy to ignore it or to fear it. Sure, she didn't know how to run a hotel. But she'd stayed in enough of them to know what she liked and didn't. That had to count for something. And her Dad had owned a popular restaurant for decades. Terri had worked there herself as a teenager and learned from her father that the key to success in the service industry was making people happy. Sounded easy, but way too many people didn't understand that.

"Just go, Terri. Grab this shiny brass ring with both hands. And if you need the cavalry, I'm only a plane ride away."

Terri grinned. "Vegas, here I come."

Four days later Terri was in Las Vegas, standing in the massive, opulent lobby of the StarFire Hotel. The floors were covered with wide, navy blue tiles that sparkled as if stars were trapped inside them. The ceiling was high and featured a night sky dazzled by twinkling stars and streaks of light from falling stars leaving trails of gold dust in their wakes. The effect was so real that if not for the crowds and the noise and the fact that it was the middle of the day, Terri would have thought she was outside staring up.

Paintings in gold inlaid frames dotted the walls, and a waiter served complimentary champagne to guests waiting in line to register. The noise level was tremendous, since the casino spilled right off the lobby. Slot machines beeped, pinged and sang out encouragement to the hundreds of people wandering the casino floor.

She turned in a slow circle, saw a gift shop, signs for restaurants and bars and still more people. From what Terri could see, the hotel seemed to stretch on forever. The outside had been impressive, but the inside was like walking into a different world.

One that was hers now.

That thought had her smiling and biting her lip at the same time. She hadn't contacted her new partner, but she had made a reservation, so she dutifully joined the tail end of the line and accepted a flute of champagne from the waiter.

She hadn't told Cooper Hayes she was coming. Terri had wanted a little time on her own, to check out her inheritance. To get a feel for what could be her new life. Or to at least explore the possibilities.

She owed that much to herself and to her parents. They'd raised her to be strong and confident. They'd sent her to college, encouraged her to find her passion. How could she walk away from this without even trying to make it work?

And in a way, didn't she owe it to her biological father, too? She hadn't known him, but he'd clearly kept track of her. He'd left her everything he had, so she was really his legacy, wasn't she?

The line moved quickly and in minutes Terri was at the desk, handing over her ID to the clerk. He was young, with a practiced smile and a name tag that read *Brent*.

"Is this your first time at the StarFire?" he asked.

Terri grinned. "How could you tell?"

He winked at her. "You keep looking up at the ceiling."

"Guilty." She took a sip of the champagne. "It's beautiful."

"It really is." He glanced at her driver's license, tapped a few keys on his keyboard then stopped, turned and stared at her as if she had three heads. "Terri Ferguson?"

"That's right." She frowned a little and tried to get a glimpse of the computer screen. "You've got my reservation, don't you?"

"Yes, ma'am," he said with the crispness of an audible salute. Gone was the easy, flirtatious smile. Brent was suddenly all business. "We've been expecting you, ma'am."

When did she become *ma'am*? "Expecting me?" She'd hoped to fly in under the radar but apparently that wasn't going to happen.

"Your suite is prepared and ready for you, Ms. Ferguson."

"I didn't reserve a suite," she said.

He grinned, printed off two key cards and slid them into a folder with the word *StarFire* emblazoned across it. He returned her ID, handed her the keys, then looked up and waved to someone behind her. "Like I said, Mr. Hayes—and we—have been expecting you."

"He has?" *Well, of course he has, Terri.* Hadn't the lawyer told her as much?

"Your name was tagged in the system so we'd recognize your arrival right away." Brent smiled again. "Your suite's been ready for days. Bill here will take your bags—"

A bellman in his twenties appeared out of nowhere beside her.

"Oh, I've only got the one bag, and it has wheels. I can—"

"It's my job, Ms. Ferguson," Bill said. "I'll show you to your suite."

Of course they'd reserved a suite. Terri had never stayed in a hotel like this one—let alone in a suite. This was so far out of her everyday ballpark, she couldn't even see the stadium from here. But she was part owner now of this amazing hotel, so she'd better get used to it. Right, and that didn't feel weird at all.

"Okay." She swallowed the last of her champagne and slid the glass across the counter to Brent. "Could you take care of this please?"

"My pleasure, Ms. Ferguson. And welcome to StarFire."

Welcome. She followed Bill across the polished lake of a floor toward a bank of elevators. Terri didn't feel welcome. She felt…on edge. She was about to meet her new partner. About to start a life that she had zero experience with. In a place she didn't know with people who were strangers. Sure. Great. Nerves? No, who would have nerves?

Everything had changed so quickly, she'd hardly had time to take a breath, and now she was in Las Vegas taking the first step into a world she didn't belong in.

Now the question was, could she make a place for herself here? Would Cooper Hayes try to stand in her way? And if he did, was she willing to fight for a new life? Instantly, she thought of all the things she could do with the inheritance her father had left her. She could buy a house, send her mom and aunt on a trip around the world if they wanted it.

The possibilities were endless. All she had to do was prove she could fit in. Be a part of this world. This business.

In her head, she heard her friend Jan saying, "Go for it, Terri. Enjoy it. Life just got way interesting."

Besides, Terri told herself, it was too late to back out now.

That last thought had barely raced through her mind when she saw *him*.

It was as if the crowds melted away. The ambient noise was nothing more than a buzz in her ears. Her heart pounded, her mouth went dry and her gaze locked on what was probably the most gorgeous man she'd ever seen in her life.

Every cell inside her stood up and started cheering. Honestly, even from a distance, he had the kind of magnetism that could turn a woman's knees to jelly. He stood alone, tall and invincible as people hurried past him, instinctively giving him a wide berth. He wore a black suit with a shirt so white it was nearly blinding against the dark red tie. His black hair was expertly shaggy and his eyes were a pale, clear blue so startling, she couldn't look away.

He was watching her, too, but she couldn't tell what he was thinking by the expression on his face. Not surprising, she supposed. A billionaire businessman—especially one who owned casinos—like Cooper Hayes—was probably born with a poker face.

Cooper Hayes. Her new partner.

And a man who could feed her fantasies forever.

Two

Dave Carey watched the security footage from his office. He'd gotten a text alert the moment Terri Ferguson's name had been entered into the hotel computers. She was here and now he had to find a way to get her gone.

He watched her now on the screen, a cold fist in the pit of his stomach. From his computer he could tap into any camera in the hotel. As executive assistant to Cooper Hayes, Dave pretty much had the run of the place. And it paid to always be on top of whatever was happening in the casino.

"She's hotter than I expected," he muttered, studying the footage of Terri Ferguson as she spoke to Cooper. "That's not good."

Cooper might think of himself as having a great poker face, but Dave had known the man since college.

He could tell in a blink that Cooper was intrigued by his new partner. And that wasn't good for Dave.

Hell, none of this was.

He tossed a pen onto his desk, leaned back in his black leather chair and kept his gaze locked on the tall blonde who had ruined his plans. Why couldn't she have been short and ugly with an overbite and a dragging limp or something? No, she had to look like a damn goddess. Who would have guessed that women in a wilderness like *Utah* could look that good? He watched her smile at Cooper and more important, watched Cooper give her that *hungry-lion-looking-at-a-gazelle* expression.

"Damn it." After years of putting in the time, helping Cooper build the Hayes Corporation into a global power, Dave had been on the cusp of finally getting what he deserved. Cooper had promised Dave that soon his loyalty would finally be rewarded.

And now some country-bumpkin blonde with great legs and a spectacular rack put it all in jeopardy.

Standing, Dave walked away from the image of Cooper staring at Terri Ferguson as if he were trying to keep from taking a bite of her. Moving across his office, Dave didn't notice the high-end furniture, the thick carpets strewn across hardwood floors. He didn't even see the wide windows giving him an awesome view of Vegas and the desert and mountains beyond. Instead, his mind was dredging up a meeting with Cooper nearly two years ago.

"Jacob's not getting any younger, you know. And when he dies, the company comes to me. Once I'm fully in charge," Cooper had said, lifting a glass of scotch in a toast, "I'll see to it that you get a major chunk of Hayes Corp."

Pleased, Dave had instantly wanted to know exactly how much they were talking about. But he came at the question subtly. "I appreciate it, Coop," he said, "but what are you really saying?"

"I'm saying that you've had nearly as big a hand as I have, turning the company into what it is today," Cooper said and Dave silently agreed. He was the one, after all, who ran around setting up meetings, taking care of minor issues before they became big ones and in general doing whatever Cooper didn't have the time to handle.

"I couldn't have accomplished so much so quickly if I hadn't been able to count on you." Cooper took a sip of his Scotch, then set it down again.

"That's good to hear," Dave said, nodding. Lifting his own glass, he took a sip and gave a quick glance around Cooper's private suite. It was palatial and, as always, Dave felt a swift, hard stab of envy that he was just barely able to disguise. He was paid very well and still he couldn't come close to living as Cooper did.

And damn it, he wanted to.

Dave's parents had worked hard all their lives and never got anywhere. They hadn't been able to help him with college. He'd put himself through and getting Cooper Hayes as a roommate had just been a damn bonus. Dave had gotten close to Cooper and slowly cut ties with his blue-collar family as he began to move in higher, glossier circles. By the time he graduated and went to work at Hayes along with Cooper, Dave had turned his back on his own past completely, in favor of his future.

Hell, he hadn't seen his family in more than ten years and if anyone asked about them, Dave kept it simple and told people they were all dead. Easier that way.

"I'm going to want to make some changes once I have unilateral power. Jacob doesn't see things the way I do. He thinks one hotel in London is sufficient. But why have one when you can have two or three?"

Musing aloud, Cooper said again, "Once I'm in charge, everything will change."

"Well, that turned out to be true, anyway," Dave muttered, slapping one hand to the window glass, warm from the October sun. This woman's arrival had ruined everything. Now Cooper had a partner again. He wasn't completely in charge and wouldn't be unless they could get rid of Terri Ferguson. And until that happened, Dave wouldn't get what he'd been working toward for more than ten years.

Oh, he knew that Cooper's plan was to get little Miss Utah out of Vegas as quickly as possible. But Dave wasn't fooling himself about this. He'd seen the interest on Cooper's face as he looked at Terri Ferguson. And if Cooper was that attracted, the urgency to chase the woman off would fade. Pretty soon she'd be settled in, making plans, and Dave's plans would be completely obliterated.

Pushing away from the window, he stalked back to his desk and sat down to stare at the image of the blonde who had, just by being here, become his enemy.

As Cooper and Terri disappeared into the elevator, Dave shut down the surveillance feed. There were no cameras in the private elevator or the owner's floor so there was no point in trying to track them.

Alone with his thoughts again, Dave's mind raced with plans, possibilities. He had to find a way to get rid of Terri Ferguson and make it look like leaving was her own idea. He had to convince the gorgeous blonde that she was out of her depth. It wouldn't be easy, of course. But Dave had handled tough assignments for years.

He could handle this, too.

But first, he told himself, it was time to call out the Big Guns, and he reached for the phone.

She wasn't what Cooper had expected.

His own fault, really. He could have done research on her. He'd handed that off to Dave and then never followed up. Mainly because he hadn't wanted to even *think* about having to deal with a new partner, for God's sake. If he had done due diligence, he might have been prepared for his first sight of her.

The world he traveled in was populated by celebrities, wealthy business people and other so-called "elites." When he'd heard that his new partner, Terri Ferguson, was a bank teller from Utah, somehow he'd expected…less. He wasn't even sure what, really. Only that Terri was more—much more—than he'd imagined.

She filled his vision to the point of shutting out everything else. She was tall, which he appreciated. He'd always hated bending nearly in half to look a woman in the eye or to kiss her senseless. This woman probably stood five feet eight inches without the three-inch black heels she wore. Her dress was a deep, rich blue that hugged curves designed to drive a man crazy. The swirling hem of her dress stopped well above her knees, displaying long, shapely legs that were toned and tanned. The bodice was cut low enough to be tempting and she wore a black shrug sweater against the October chill.

Her long blond hair tumbled across her shoulders and down her back in thick, heavy waves and her summer-blue eyes were pinned on him. Just for a second, he indulged himself with another look at the full, rich curve of her breasts and his body stirred in response. Damn it. She was beautiful.

And a distraction he didn't want or need, he reminded himself.

The only reason she was there, in his hotel, was to throw a monkey wrench into the middle of Cooper's business plans. So it didn't matter what she looked like, or that his body was tight and uncomfortable just looking at her. All that mattered was that he get her to sign over her half of the business in exchange for the huge buyout he was willing to offer her.

The bellman skidded to a stop when he spotted Cooper. "Mr. Hayes. I was just showing Ms. Ferguson to her suite, sir."

"So I see." Cooper took two long steps forward and stopped right in front of her. He was close enough to see the flash of something…interesting in her eyes. To hear the quick intake of breath and to notice how she squared her shoulders as if preparing for battle. Which, whether she knew it or not, he told himself, was the right reaction to this situation.

"You're Cooper Hayes," she said and he deliberately refused to notice the low pitch of her voice. Decided to not wonder how that voice would sound as a whisper in the darkness.

"I am," he said. "I've been expecting you."

Bill stood there, swiveling his head back and forth, watching the two of them as if he was at a tennis match.

"Sorry I'm late?" She smiled with the question and her eyes lit up. Completely irrelevant.

"You're not late. I just thought you would arrive sooner than you did."

Cooper noticed the bellman now getting even more interested in the conversation and he had no interest in supplying his employees with entertainment. Fixing his gaze on the younger man, he said, "I'll take it from here, thanks."

"Yes, sir." Bill shot Terri what Cooper thought of as a sympathetic glance, then Bill turned and hurried back to the main lobby.

"Wow, he moved fast." Terri sent a quick look over her shoulder. "Do you inspire fear in all your employees?"

"Not fear," he corrected. "Respect."

"Oh, of course. Wide eyes and a dead run are sure signs of respect."

He took a breath. Apparently, she'd be harder to intimidate than the people who worked for him. "Are we going to talk about the bellman, or would you like to see your suite?"

Terri grinned. "I can do both."

"Why am I not surprised?" he muttered. Gripping the suitcase handle with one hand, he placed the other at the small of her back, turning her toward the bank of elevators and one that stood alone, separate from the rest.

"Anyway," she said, turning her head to take in the expansive casino behind them, "I'd have been here sooner, but there was a lot to do. I had to put in for a leave of absence at my job, get my car checked to make sure it was safe for the drive—"

"You drove?" He interrupted the flow of words because he was pretty sure that was the only chance he'd have to speak at all. "If you had called to let us know you were coming, I'd have sent the jet for you."

"You have your own jet?" she asked, goggling at him.

"*We* do."

"*We* have a jet. Right. Who doesn't?" Shaking her head, she took a breath and said, "Anyway, I drove so I could stop off in St. George to see my mom and my aunt. Tell them what had happened and get them to babysit my dog for me because I didn't know how long I'd be gone and I couldn't ask my friend to watch her for who knows how many days—"

"You have a dog?" Cooper didn't know why that hit him, but it did. It was something that hadn't come up in Dave's research, either. Cooper'd never had a dog. Or a cat. Or hell, even a hamster. Growing up in a hotel didn't lend itself to pets. As a kid, that had bothered him. Apparently, it still did.

She grinned. "Yes. Daisy's a cute mix of about a hundred and fifty different breeds, and she thinks she's a Great Dane, so she needs a lot of attention and really doesn't like being left alone. My mom loves her, so Daisy's happy and—"

"What did your mom say about all of this?" Another interruption and he didn't feel the slightest bit guilty about it. Until she spoke.

"You keep interrupting me. That's rude, you know, but it's okay for now."

"Thanks so much," he said wryly, but she apparently didn't catch the sarcasm.

"Mom's as freaked out by this as I am," Terri continued. "Neither of us knew anything about my biological parents so we're kind of shocked to find out my birth father even knew who I was, let alone *where* I was. Sorry. Rambling. The point is, I had a few things to take care of before I could come to Vegas."

That bright, brilliant smile had knocked him back for a second but thankfully she hadn't noticed. He felt off his game and that was something Cooper couldn't afford. With that firmly in mind, he brushed aside her rambling. "Doesn't matter. You're here now." Nodding, he slid a card into the slot of the stand-alone elevator. "This is a private elevator. It's the one you'll use to get to and from your suite. The other elevators stop at the nineteenth floor. This one goes directly to the top five floors and the roof."

"Okay…" Another deep breath and he refused to notice how her breasts lifted with the action.

Focusing had never been an issue for Cooper. Until today, apparently.

"The waitstaff and housekeeping have their own elevators that will take them to the top floors for business purposes. The general public can't access the higher floors."

"Sounds very…secure."

If she was joking he let her know by his tone that he didn't find it funny. "As secure as technology can make it. Hayes Corporation offices are on the twentieth floor," he said, turning his focus from her to the matter at hand. "And on twenty-one, two and three we have suites for special guests, dignitaries, celebrities… anyone whose security issues demand a safe, impregnable, luxury suite."

"Impregnable. Right. Sounds cozy." She nodded as the elevator doors whisked open.

"Our guests don't come here for 'cozy.'"

"Good thing," she murmured.

He took that as a direct insult. "A cozy hotel is a B and B. A Hayes hotel offers luxury. Exclusivity."

She blinked at him. "Wow. That sounds terrible."

Surprised again, he said, "What about that is terrible?"

"Oh, just everything, but never mind…"

Cooper thought about arguing her ridiculous point but buried his irritation instead. Unknowingly, she was proving that he was right to want to buy her out of this partnership. If she didn't understand the basics of the hotel industry, then she had no business being a partner. Certainly not *his* partner.

He took a breath. "The owners' suites are on the twenty-fourth floor." Cooper steered her inside the open elevator, slid his card into the slot again, pushed the right button and stood back, looking at her. With the mirrored wall behind her, he was able to take her all in at once. And he had to admit, every damn view he got of her was a good one.

Too bad she was such a pain in the ass.

The elevator swept up in a rush and she laughed, a rich, deep bubble of sound that whipped through the small, enclosed space and wrapped itself around his throat until Cooper felt like he couldn't breathe. Pure enjoyment wreathed her features, when only a moment or two before, she'd been irritated, and damned if he wasn't…captivated. Most women he knew were more guarded about their emotions. But Terri was honest and open and he found that intriguing.

She grabbed hold of the brass rail at her side, tossed her hair back and slanted him a delighted glance. "Well, that's faster than I expected."

"Express elevator." His own voice sounded as tight as he felt. Cooper watched her staring up at the elevator roof and realized she was the first woman he'd been with in this elevator who didn't turn and check herself out in the mirror. Every female he knew would fluff her hair or smooth her lipstick or simply give her appearance a mental thumbs-up. Terri Ferguson, though, was looking up at the digital midnight sky.

"That's so fabulous. Like the lobby." She shook her head. "I love the shooting stars. It looks so real."

"I wouldn't know. Living in a city with this much ambient light, you don't see many stars."

She leveled her gaze on him. "Now, that's a shame."

"I've never thought so."

"Then you don't know what you're missing," she said, looking at him with what could only be sympathy.

Well, Cooper Hayes didn't need anyone to feel sorry for him. Especially over something as minor as not being a stargazer. Watching her, he figured this was just one example of how the two of them were from different worlds. She looked at the stars in the sky, and the only stars he was interested in were the celebrities who came to his hotels. Yeah, a partnership between them would be doomed. Best to end it as soon as possible.

She turned her gaze back to the ceiling, a soft smile on her face, when falling stars left trails of gold dust across a digital sky. Cooper didn't bother looking at the illusion. Instead, he watched her pleased smile and wondered why the hell he was enjoying it.

Deliberately, he brushed it off and started talking. "We work with a company who designs and installs illusionist skies in the hallways, casino, the lobby. StarFire can follow you all over the hotel."

"That's amazing. I'm a little technologically challenged, so imagining people who can do that? Wow." She looked at him. "It's really great. I mean, everything I've seen since I walked in the door has been just beautiful."

Her face was open and easy to read. So he saw her excitement, the touch of nerves in the way her teeth tugged at her bottom lip. The easy curve of that smile did things to him he really didn't want to think about. Irritated, he snapped, "Glad you approve."

And just like that, her smile wobbled and her eyes lost that sparkle.

Idiot.

Being charming with a beautiful woman had never been difficult for him. Before Terri Ferguson, apparently.

He spoke up again quickly. "The illusions are relatively new. Installed just a couple years ago, but everyone seems to like them."

"I can see why." She relaxed again, but her eyes still looked wary, as if she had walls up because she'd wandered into a hotbed of enemies. Which he really didn't want her to be thinking. He needed her to see him not as an enemy, but rather as a man who was going to do her the favor of sparing her all the work necessary to keep a company like Hayes Corporation running.

"You said yourself this was a strange situation to be in," he reminded her with a deliberately casual shrug. "Well, I only found out about *you* a few days ago, too."

She blinked at him. "Jacob never said anything about me?"

"No. I didn't find out the truth until a few hours before you did. So now we're both surprised." He tapped one finger on the key card folder she held. "Anyway, your card will take you to any of the top floors. Right now I'm showing you to your owner's suite."

She dragged in another breath, tossed her hair back over her shoulder and tightened her grip on the cold, brass rail. "Is that where my father stayed?"

"Only when he was in town. He mainly lived in New York."

Even to him, his voice sounded cool, disinterested— and that wasn't good. If Cooper's plan was to smooth the way for her to become an in-name-only partner, then he needed to be a hell of a lot more amiable than he'd managed to be so far. It shouldn't have been difficult at all, but his attraction to her was throwing him off balance. Not something Cooper enjoyed. "Jacob wasn't in Vegas often over the last couple of years, so I didn't see much of him. And I would have, since I live here in the hotel."

Her gaze snapped to his. "You do?"

He'd surprised her and he supposed he could understand it. In her world, people probably lived in neat little houses with backyards and dogs and kids. People *visited* hotels; they didn't live there.

"I practically grew up here," he told her. "Always figured to move out eventually. Get a place away from the Strip, but I realized I like the Strip. And living here is easy. My office is right downstairs. Twenty-four-hour room service, and housekeeping."

"Sure. Of course. Well, housekeeping I really understand. That would be handy." She laughed a little and he heard the nerves in it. "Sorry." She held up one hand and shook her head, smiling wryly. "This is hard to take in. Last week I juggled bills so I could pay to have my car fixed and now..."

"Now you can buy any car you want."

She blew out a breath. "That hasn't really settled in yet."

"Get used to it," Cooper advised quietly.

This was good. He wanted her to realize that the money she'd inherited could change her life. He wanted her to go out and play, explore the world. Hell, do *anything* but stay in Vegas and try to help him run *his* company.

"Your old world is over." When the elevator doors opened with a whoosh, he added, "Welcome to your new one."

A wide hallway where the sun shone through several skylights plugged into the ceiling stretched out on either side of the elevator. Pale blue carpet covered the floor, and the soft gray walls held framed photos of different hotels in the Hayes chain. Cooper watched her take it all in and felt a flush of pride. He was so used to his surroundings, he rarely noticed any of it. But her reaction to the place made him pause briefly to enjoy what he'd built.

"So many different hotels," she murmured, walking up to the closest painting. It was the villa in Tuscany that boasted views from every room and a world-class spa.

"We're in hundreds of countries," he said, not without a touch of pride.

She turned her head to look up at him. "I hate to keep using the word *amazing*, but it's the only one that seems to fit." Then she looked up and down the sunlit hall. "Well, this is different. I'm used to narrow, dark hotel hallways."

"None of our hotels have dark hallways," he said and

saw a flash in her eyes at his use of the word *our*. "Not good for business. Makes guests nervous."

"But no StarFire skies up here? The illusions, I mean?"

"The illusions are for the tourists. Our guests. I prefer reality." He glanced at the skylights and the sunlight pouring through. "I wanted real light up here. Feels less closed in this way."

Pushing her hair back from her face, she asked, "Do you always speak in short sentences?"

"What?"

She smirked and he ground his teeth together. Fine. He did tend to speak with as few words as possible. Saved time. But no one had ever called him on it before. "Are you always so blunt?"

"Usually," she said, turning to look up and down the hallway. "It's easier to just be up front and honest. Lies tend to get all tangled and twisted."

Now it was his turn to smirk. "Honesty may be best in Utah, but it's not really popular in Vegas. Not exactly the way most business deals are made."

"That's too bad," she said, then tipped her head to one side, her long, blond hair sliding off her shoulders to shine in the sun pouring through the skylight above. "Don't you think?"

"Never thought about it."

"Maybe you should." She squared her shoulders again. She was still preparing for battle. "So, which way?"

He pointed down the hall behind her. "Your suite's to the left of the elevator."

She inhaled sharply and he took a moment to enjoy the lift of her breasts. Damn, he really was spending way too much time thinking about her body and wanting to see more of it. Preferably naked, spread across his bed with moonlight streaming through the windows. But he got a grip on the daydreams and deliberately pushed them aside. Yes, she was gorgeous, but he wasn't going to get involved with the woman he was trying to get rid of. That would only complicate things further.

When Cooper had heard Jacob's daughter was from Utah, Cooper had made the stupid assumption that she'd be some unsophisticated farm girl or something. And for that, he wanted to kick himself. He should have known better than to make assumptions. Maybe he should get out of Vegas once in a while.

As she walked down the hall in front of him, Cooper enjoyed the view. Her long legs made him wish they were wrapped around his hips, and her butt was a work of art. Her hair swung from side to side with every step she took, and her hips swayed in a silent invitation he was more than ready to accept. She flipped him a look over her shoulder and he saw how the dark blue dress she wore reflected in her eyes, making them a startling, crystal blue. Then she smiled and he felt the jolt of it slam home.

She was fascinating. More so than he'd thought she'd be.

More than he could afford to acknowledge.

Whatever he wanted to do to her, with her, he had

to remember, she didn't belong here and if he had his way, she wouldn't be staying.

He thought of what little information Dave had found on her—only child, father deceased. Well, they shared that, anyway. She'd graduated from Weber State College with a degree in archaeology—as if that would come in handy in the hotel business. She lived alone in a condo she made regular payments on and worked at a bank as a teller and new accounts executive.

That was it. No dirt. No gossip. No angry ex-lover who made threats. No arrests, not even for jaywalking. She was so good it was almost eerie.

This kind of woman was not made for Vegas.

Which meant she wasn't for him, either.

At the suite door, she took one of her midnight blue key cards from the folder and pushed it into the slot. Cooper stayed back, wanting to watch her reaction as she stepped into the luxurious owner's suite.

He wasn't disappointed.

She gave an audible sigh at her first sight of the place and stopped so suddenly to take it all in that he almost ran into her. "This is…"

"Amazing?"

She turned and gave him a quick grin. "Yes. Absolutely."

Cooper walked around her and left her pink—of course it was pink—suitcase against the wall. He edged his suit jacket back and tucked both hands into his pockets.

Still watching her expression, he said, "It's a three-bedroom, three-bath suite. There's no kitchen, but there is a coffee bar that's restocked every evening and a bar fridge with soft drinks, water and wine. The wet bar is across the room and if there's a type of liquor you prefer and can't find it, call downstairs and they'll bring it to you."

"Of course they will."

He wasn't sure what she meant by that, but ignored it and moved on. "There are snacks in the fridge, too, but room service will bring you anything you want any time of day."

"Right." She nodded, letting her gaze slide around the room.

He did the same. The suites had been updated and redecorated only a year ago. Jacob's decorator had gone with shades of gray and smoky blue. There was plenty of chrome, lots of glass and wide-planked hardwood floors dotted with plush throw rugs. The balcony outside a pair of French doors ran the width of the building, affording both Terri and Cooper access.

"This is amazing," she whispered.

"There's that word again," he mused with a chuckle. If she was this blown away by her own suite, it shouldn't take long at all to convince her that she was completely out of her depth as a partner in this business. That was good, wasn't' it? Get rid of her quickly—especially because of what she was doing to him. "Follow me. I'll show you the rest of the place."

"Oh." She spun around to look at him and her eyes were wide. "You don't have to do that. You probably have more important things to do."

He did. But he wanted to get a better feel for her and

what she was thinking, feeling. And, as long as he was being honest with himself, he could silently admit that he liked looking at her. "Not at the moment."

"Okay, then."

Cooper closed the roller handle and simply carried her suitcase down a hall to the first of three bedrooms. He opened the door, stepped inside, then moved back to watch her again. Really, he'd never known anyone with such an expressive face. Her delight was clearly stamped on her features, and her eyes were sparkling. Maybe it was growing up in the business world. Or maybe it was Vegas itself, but it seemed that everyone constantly hid what they were thinking or feeling. As if letting anyone in meant giving away their edge.

And truth be told, that was how Cooper operated, as well. He'd spent most of his life building the walls that surrounded him. As a businessman, he kept what he was thinking, what he was after, under lock and key. The only one he truly felt he could be honest with was Dave. Everyone else was kept at a safe distance.

A woman as open and honest as Terri Ferguson was a risk to the walls Cooper had spent a lifetime building.

"This is amazing. Really." She spun around to face him and pleasure was stamped on her features. "I swear I'm going to find another word to use. Once I get used to—" she waved her arms to encompass the lovely room "—all of this. Shouldn't take more than a year or two."

You won't be here that long.

Yet, even as he thought it, he responded to the shine in her eyes, the wide smile on her face and he thought of things they could do together that would get the same reactions from her. Hell, he could practically taste that mouth of hers. She did a quick spin in place and the hem of her dress lifted higher above her knees, giving him one brief glimpse of smooth, strong thighs.

Instantly, he shut those thoughts down. He didn't need them. Didn't want them. And, he half resented that not only had she arrived to stick her nose in his business, but she was, without even trying, turning his dick to stone.

"Settle in. We'll talk later." His voice sounded gruff even to him. And a part of his brain quietly whispered, *Charming, remember?*

But screw that. He'd used up his daily quota of charm. He looked into her eyes and felt his world tip and he didn't like it. Best to leave now. He wanted to get out of there while he could still walk.

"Okay, then," she said, already turning away from him to wander into the adjoining bath. "I'll see you later."

"Right." Fine. Hell.

She didn't even watch him leave.

Three

Terri didn't stay in the beautiful room for long. Sure, if she'd been on vacation, she would have indulged herself in the luxury of it all for hours. But then again, if she was on vacation, she wouldn't have a room like this. The place she could afford would be a motel somewhere off the Strip probably sandwiched between a liquor store and a pawn shop.

But today, instead, she was staying at the top of a palace.

Her mother had made her promise to take pictures of the hotel so Terri had already documented most of the suite. Now she took some pictures in the grand bathroom.

"Wow. Just...*wow*," she murmured as she moved her phone around to catch the whole thing. From the seafoam-colored tiles to the shower that took up one end of the room with multiple nozzles and a bench—she supposed it was there for when you got exhausted just walking back and forth to the shampoo alcove.

The pale green marble counter was stocked with shampoos and lotions and towels so fluffy and huge they almost qualified as blankets. She still could hardly believe this was happening to her.

"I've never even seen a tub that big," she muttered, taking a picture of the deep soaker tub almost as big as a pool and complete with jets. She couldn't wait to try it out.

"Later," she promised herself and gave a quick look at the mirror, checking her reflection.

Her heart was beating a little fast; her eyes looked wider than normal with a sheen of excitement in them she hadn't seen in a long time. Was it for this place, what was happening in her life?

Or was it, she wondered, because of Cooper Hayes himself?

As if in answer, her heartbeat sped up even faster and her breath caught in her throat.

It was more than just the way he looked, which was off-the-charts gorgeous—but there was an aura of power about him that fascinated her. He was steely and strong and the way he bit words off made her long to hear more of that deep voice. Not to mention the fact that when he touched her, she felt a kind of heat she'd never experienced before.

Not a good thing right now, she reminded herself. She needed to get used to this new world. To see if she could make it her own. Getting involved with her new partner wasn't a smart plan. Then you were tangling up business and need and something was bound to go wrong.

Wow, this was not something she'd expected. Of course, here she was in a plush suite with a lap-pool bathtub and a view of Las Vegas that usually only birds saw. So what about this *was* expected? Then she remembered the flash of something dangerous in Cooper's eyes as he looked at her and told herself that this was a man she had no idea how to handle. But she'd love the chance to *try* handling him.

"Okay, get a grip," she told the woman in the mirror. "You're not here for a romance. You're here because—" She stopped.

Because her old life wasn't enough. Yes, she'd been happy, but now there was a chance at adventure. At something bigger than she'd ever dreamed. She wanted to make this work, she realized. And once her mind was made up, as her Dad used to say, there was just no stopping Terri Ferguson.

Grabbing her black leather bag, she slung it over her left shoulder and headed for the door. The elevator ride was fast. She was still wearing the dark blue dress she'd arrived in and thought she looked pretty good for taking her first self-guided tour of the casino. When the doors swished open, a wall of noise erupted that shocked Terri even as it drew her in.

Stepping off the elevator, she was instantly pulled into the humming pulse of the crowd. It wasn't the first time Terri had been to a casino, of course. Wendover, Nevada, was only a two-hour drive from Ogden so she and Jan often made the drive to see a show or spend the weekend at slot machines, trying to win a fortune that would change their lives.

Well, now her life *had* been changed and so she was looking at this immense adult playground with new eyes, hoping it would give her some kind of insight into her new *partner*.

The place was beautiful, of course. Like the rest of the hotel, the StarFire theme wended its way through the casino, as well. There were slot machines with flashing images of stars sailing through a night sky, and the illusion ceiling stretched across the entire room. The carpet was a deep, midnight blue with silver threads peppering it so that it looked like a night sky, as well. Mirrors dotted the walls and row after row of beeping, clanging machines with eager tourists perched in front of them stood on the carpet like soldiers. Table games formed a huge circle in the center of the casino, and overhead there was another illusion sky, this one with planets and shooting stars making a dramatic statement.

Terri wandered, wanting to see it all—not just the hotel and casino itself, but the guests—how they were being treated, if they looked happy. Like at her Dad's restaurant, the best way to tell if a business was in good shape was to judge it from the customer's point of view. From what she could see, everyone seemed to be having a great time. It was late afternoon, though there were no clocks in the casino to announce that fact.

Music streamed from a lounge bar where the night theme included black-topped tables and pinpoint lights on the walls. Powerful fans ensured there was only a faint hint of cigarette smoke in the air. Cocktail waitresses in impossibly high heels and body-hugging black and silver costumes hurried through the crowd, balancing trays holding full drinks and empties. Somewhere close by, a woman shrieked in excitement and bells and whistles went off at shrill levels that had Terri quickening her steps. She was still smiling as she walked away from the crowds toward what looked like a circle of peace in the madness.

A glassed-in area held sofas, chairs and pots and pots of flowers, blooms bursting in every color imaginable. There were two women inside, each of them working on their phones. Terri walked past, promising herself she'd check it out personally later. She was a little surprised the enclosed area wasn't more crowded with people looking to take a break from the noise.

For more than an hour, Terri wandered through the hotel and the surrounding grounds. She watched valets laughing with customers and then racing off to get their cars. She saw the bellmen loading carts with luggage. Hotel guests were a steady stream, coming and going. Just beyond the front of the hotel lay the famous Strip, bustling with thousands of tourists.

Her self-guided tour ended when her black heels finally began to make her feet pay. They were beautiful shoes and she loved them, but they had not been designed for hiking. She took a seat at the bar in the main casino and smiled at the bartender.

Glancing at his name tag, she said, "Brandon, I would love a glass of chardonnay."

"Right away." He was gorgeous—just like every other employee she'd noticed—and Terri wondered if good looks were a requirement to work here. He had short blond hair, kind green eyes and wore a midnight-black vest shot through with silver thread over a white button-down shirt and black slacks. As he poured, he gave her a wide smile. "Your first stay at StarFire?"

"How could you tell?" she asked. "Am I that obvious?"

He shrugged, set her glass down on the gleaming black bar top and said, "It's the way you're looking around. As if you're afraid you're going to miss something."

"In my defense, there's a lot to see." Terri took a sip and set the glass back down with a satisfied sigh. "Oh, that's good, thanks. And yes, it's my first time here. It's a beautiful place. Do you like working here?"

It wasn't just small talk; she really wanted to know how people felt about their jobs. And if she was now part owner, shouldn't she?

He shrugged, wiped down a nonexistent spot on the bar top. "No real complaints. Good pay, meet nice people—" He winked.

She smiled and had another sip of the great, icy-cold wine. "Really. I'm curious."

He planted both hands on the edge of the bar, tipped his head to one side and gave it some thought. "On the whole, sure. It's a great hotel. Classy guests. Being a bartender, you see some really weird stuff, but not so much here. It's absolutely the best place I've worked."

She was glad to hear it.

"But," he added, "it'd be nice if they were more flexible with the shifts."

"What do you mean?"

He shrugged and gave a quick look around as if to make sure no one could overhear him complaining. "They don't like us trading shifts if something comes up—like, I had to take my wife to the baby doctor for an ultrasound last week—"

"Congratulations."

"Thanks!" He gave her a wide grin and a thumbs-up. "It's our first. A girl. Anyway, I work afternoons, but I needed the late shift that day. Couldn't switch with the night bartender, so I had to lose a day of pay." He shrugged. "Things like that. It's not bad, necessarily, but it'd be good if they were more willing to work with us."

"Seems like it would make sense," she said. Terri wondered why the hotel was so rigid. As long as the shifts were covered, did it matter *which* bartender was on duty?

"Anything else?" Now that she'd gotten him talking, she wanted to hear more. Customers were a good ruler of how a business fulfilled its duties. But employees were the heartbeat of the place. If she was now a partner in this hotel—and all the others—she wanted to know what was working…and even more important, what *wasn't*.

He laughed a little. "Writing a book?"

"No, just nosy."

All around them the casino was hopping, and at the end of the bar, two men sat sipping beers and playing video poker.

"Okay, why not? This almost feels therapeutic." He had to think about it again. "Well, why can't there be cocktail *waiters* as well as waitresses? Guys could do the job, too."

"Good point," she said, wondering why no one, including her, had ever thought about it.

"And the employee break room?" He shook his head as he warmed to his theme. "Sad. One little fridge and a coffeepot. Oh, and a vending machine with cookies and chips."

"That does sound sad," she said, laughing. "Actually, it sounds like the employee break room at the bank where I work."

"Hey," Brandon said, holding out a hand. "We are survivors of mediocre food and lumpy couches."

She shook his hand and made a mental note to write down everything he'd told her. She could talk to Cooper about this next time she saw him. Wow. Was this what it felt like to be in charge? To have power?

At that thought, she nearly laughed out loud. She didn't have any power. She was a stranger in a strange land and didn't know what to do first.

"Terri Ferguson?"

Turning at the voice right behind her, Terri smiled at the man watching her. He had short blond hair, brown eyes and was wearing an exceptionally well-cut suit. "Yes, I'm Terri Ferguson."

"Nice to meet you," he said, holding out one hand. "I'm Dave Carey, Cooper's executive assistant."

"Oh." She smiled wider and shook his hand. "Nice to meet you, too."

When he released her hand, Dave looked at the bartender and said, "So, what are you and the new owner of the StarFire talking about?"

"New owner?" Brandon's voice was soft, worried. "Terri Ferguson. They told us you'd be arriving soon. I'm sorry, I didn't know—"

"There's no way you could have known, Brandon," she said, trying to ease the panic in his eyes.

"Is there a problem?" Dave asked, shifting his gaze back and forth as if sensing the sudden tension.

"No, of course not," Terri said quickly. No doubt Brandon was frantically rethinking their conversation and wondering if he'd said something that was going to turn around and bite him. His gaze shifted briefly to Dave then back to her with a silent plea in his eyes and she knew he'd rather she didn't mention what they'd been talking about.

Smiling, she turned to Dave. "Brandon's been really helpful. He was just telling me about the movie theater on the third floor." She shook her head. "Apparently, I didn't get far enough in my wandering. I couldn't believe you have your own theater."

"It's not my theater now, Ms. Ferguson. It's yours."

"Terri, please," she said and ignored what he'd said. Until she got accustomed to all of this it was easier on her to not really acknowledge that she was an owner of this fabulous place. "So, how did you know where to find me?"

Dave eased onto a bar stool, then pointed to several spots along the ceiling. "Wasn't difficult. Surveillance cameras. They're all over the hotel and casino."

Cameras. Of course. She hadn't considered that and she should have. Honestly, even the bank in Ogden had security cams everywhere but the bathrooms. Naturally, a luxury hotel with a crowded casino would have cameras everywhere. Why hadn't she considered that earlier? She'd thought it was her secret that she'd wandered all over the hotel. Now she knew Dave had seen her. Had Cooper watched her, too? Had he bothered to look?

Perfect. A minute ago she'd hated the idea of Dave watching her every move and now she was disappointed thinking that Cooper hadn't? She didn't need to be thinking about Cooper right now.

"So you have been observing me the whole time? That's a little creepy."

Brandon moved off to serve another customer, but not before sending Terri a quiet *thank you* with his eyes.

"You make it sound like I'm a stalker," Dave said with a disarming smile. "You can relax on that score. I happened to be going over a security issue and saw you sitting here at the main bar. Thought I'd take the opportunity to meet you in person."

Okay, that made sense and eased that deer-in-the-headlights feel that had briefly gripped her. Terri laughed. "I guess you are a little busy to be watching me meander through the casino."

"Never too busy to watch a pretty woman," he said, then quickly added, "in a nonstalker way."

Smiling, and relaxing in his company, Terri picked up her wine and took a sip. "I appreciate that. But it's still a little creepy to have so many cameras documenting everything that happens. I mean, I get why they're needed, it's just…"

Dave nodded sagely. "I understand. It seems these days that there are always tiny incursions on privacy."

"Exactly." It was a shame Cooper Hayes wasn't as easy to talk to as his assistant. And it was a shame that Dave Carey didn't give her the same tingles that Cooper did.

"Still, I think most people are willing to put up with creepy if it means they feel safer."

"I suppose," Terri agreed. "Or maybe it's because they don't really look up and notice those cameras focused down on them."

"Maybe you're right." He gave a shrug then changed the subject. "We'll have to have a long conversation about the pros and cons sometime. But for right now, what do you think of the StarFire?"

"It's beautiful," she admitted shamelessly. "I took a little tour of it by myself. There's way too much to see in an hour or two, but I wanted to try to get a feel for it."

"And did you? Get a feel?"

His tone was almost flirtatious and she wanted to tell him that her body was too busy burning for Cooper to be interested in someone else. Dave seemed nice, but he didn't give her the same zip of interest that Cooper had.

Terri laughed and shook her head. "I don't think that's even possible right now."

"I get it." Dave signaled to Brandon and when the bartender came back, ordered a draft beer. "It must be hard for you, coming into all of this so unexpectedly."

Was that sympathetic or patronizing? Hard to tell. But he'd been so nice, Terri gave him the benefit of the doubt. "It's very strange. In so many ways I can't even count them all. I think my mom's in even deeper shock than I am."

"Your adoptive mother didn't know who your birth father was?"

"Nope. There weren't a lot of open adoptions twenty-eight years ago. She and my dad were just glad to get me." Terri thought about that for a long second or two, then smiled at Dave. "I have a wonderful family. Jacob Evans did me a big favor by putting me up for adoption."

Reaching out, he gave her hand a quick squeeze, then released her. *Nope, no zip of heat. Too bad, she thought. An attraction to Dave would have been much easier to deal with.*

"I'm sure he would have been glad to know it."

A pang of regret for the man she'd never know echoed inside her. "Did you know Jacob well?"

"Oh, yes. For more than a decade." Dave took a sip of his beer. "He wasn't an easy man, but he was a brilliant businessman. I think Cooper will miss his input." He paused then said, "But you'll be able to step into your father's shoes there, won't you? I mean, taking on his responsibilities in the company."

Nerve wracking words, but Terri was up for it. She was a fast learner. Stepping into upper management position at such a well-established company wouldn't be easy. But it wasn't impossible, either.

"It's a lot," she said, lifting her wineglass for another sip. "But I'll catch on."

"Oh, of course you will," Dave said. "No one expects you to know everything right away. And I'm happy to help any way I can."

"Thanks. I appreciate that." Terri took another sip and studied Dave over the rim of her glass. He was handsome, polished, friendly, but she didn't get the same *surge* of something hot and tempting from him as she did from Cooper. It would probably be much easier working with Dave, since her hormones wouldn't be distracted, so if he was willing to help her out, she'd be grateful.

"You've met Cooper, I know."

"Yes, he showed me to my suite."

"I'm impressed," he said, laughing. "Getting Cooper to take ten minutes away from the company is a real accomplishment. He gets busy, wrapped up in his work. With a corporation this size, there's always something to be handled. Some problem or challenge that has to be met. He's constantly talking about just how much work there is to do and he never stops. Which means I don't, either. Cooper expects the same kind of commitment he makes, from everyone around him." Dave glanced down the bar to where Brandon was filling a cocktail waitress's tray. "He doesn't have much time for anything but the job. So if he seems to be ignoring you, try not to take it personally." He turned back to Terri and she read sympathy in his eyes. "I'll be here, ready to stand in for Cooper whenever I can. Help ease you into your new position."

"Thank you." A workaholic partner who would expect the same from her. Well, Terri wasn't afraid of work. True, she didn't know anything at all about the hotel business, but she was smart and capable. She would learn.

And, she would prove to Cooper Hayes that she was more than just Jacob Evans's surprise daughter. If Cooper was too busy to be bothered with her, then she'd take Dave's help to find her feet here. She'd been given the chance at something wonderful—she'd be crazy to turn away from it.

Bells erupted. A woman in her sixties with short, graying blond hair and a T-shirt that read *Don't bother me, I'm reading*, shrieked and a crowd of people surrounded her as she shouted, "I won! I won! Oh, my God!"

Terri smiled at the woman's excitement and just beneath the thunderous noise, she heard Dave say, "People come from all over the world, hoping to get lucky in Las Vegas. But *you* got lucky before you even arrived, didn't you?"

She smiled at him and gave a quick look at the casino and the thousands of people milling around. It was all so new. All so promising. All she had to do was work with a man who turned her knees to jelly and carve out a role for herself in this company.

Lucky? That's how it looked, she admitted silently. But she wondered if that was really true.

Two days later Terri was alone on the balcony of her suite, watching the sun begin to set. She kept a safe distance between herself and the railing where a sheet of Plexiglas provided protection from the wind,

and still she had a spectacular view. A palace of a suite. Anything she wanted with a simple phone call to room service or the concierge. And yet she couldn't settle. Couldn't make herself relax on the couch, lose herself in a movie, relax in that glory of a tub. Heck, she couldn't even call Jan. Her insides were jumpy; her mind was racing. And nothing was going to ease it.

For two days she'd immersed herself in the hotel business. There was so much she didn't know, it was staggering. Dave had been as good as his word. He'd taken her to the office floor and introduced her to so many people, their faces became a blur and their names forgotten almost as soon as she heard them.

She'd sat in on a planning meeting and tried to keep her mind on what was being discussed while meeting Cooper's icy gaze. He had studied her as if trying to figure her out, then as soon as the meeting was over, he disappeared rather than spend any one-on-one time with her. Which irritated her on so many levels Terri couldn't begin to count them all. If not for Dave Carey, Terri would still be wandering aimlessly through her new life.

Her brain was filled with things she'd never be able to keep straight. Plans for new hotels and scheduled board meetings on expansion of a company that was already global. And she knew that she'd only seen the tip of the iceberg that was Hayes Corporation.

Nerves rattled her in spite of how kind Dave had been. Why wasn't Cooper the one to help her adjust to all of this? She was *his* partner, after all.

Why was he avoiding her?

"And more important," she murmured, "why is it bothering you that he is?"

Was he deliberately ignoring her, trying to make her so uncomfortable that she'd simply leave without learning more about her legacy? Or did he think her so unimportant she didn't rate any extra time?

"Well, either way, it's insulting," she mumbled. Curling her fingers around the wide iron railing, she let the residual heat from the metal slide into her skin while the cool October wind rushed through her hair like cold fingers. "Whether he likes it or not—heck, whether I like it or not—I'm his partner now. I think I deserve better than being ignored."

The more she thought of it, the higher the flames of her indignation flared. Had Cooper assigned Dave to her? As if she were some long lost relative to be bought off with a tour and a nice glass of wine? Was Dave patronizing her on Cooper's behalf? If that was it, Cooper was in for a surprise.

"Okay, sure, I'm not a tycoon. I don't know any-thing about the hotel business," she admitted, squeez-ing that railing. Asking herself why she hadn't gotten a degree in business instead. At least that would have served her better in this situation. Staring off at the distant mountains, watching them go purple with the sunset, she shook her head. "I'm here, though. And my…*father*…wanted me here."

Okay, that really wasn't the reason she'd come. She hadn't known her father so it felt hypocritical some-how to mourn him or to do something she didn't want to do simply to honor his wishes. She was here for her-

self. She hadn't really known that she was unsatisfied with her life before, because it was all she'd known and she'd accepted it. But now, out of the blue, she'd been handed the opportunity to completely shake up her life. How could she not at least *try*?

"I'm going to be the best partner ever and Cooper is just going to have to get used to having me around."

When a knock on the door sounded, she practically raced through the living room, desperate for *anything* to focus on besides her own whirling thoughts.

She opened the door and stopped dead. Cooper Hayes, big as life and twice as gorgeous, stood there, looking down at her. Instantly, she wished she were wearing her high heels instead of slip-on flats. Being several inches shorter than he was made her feel at a disadvantage. Of course, so did the fact that she was happy to see him—in spite of being so irritated with him only moments before—and he looked as though he wished he were anywhere but there.

"Cooper."

His black suit was tailored to perfection and he wore a midnight-blue tie shot through with silver over a white dress shirt. The tie had been loosened and the top collar button undone. For Cooper, she figured this was casual wear.

One hand braced on the door frame, he pushed the other through his hair and, fascinated, Terri watched those thick strands fall perfectly into place. She almost sighed and then wanted to kick herself for it.

"What're you doing here?"

He scrubbed one hand across his face. "I wanted to talk to you."

"Why the change? You've ignored me for two days."

He scowled. "I was working."

"Right. And now all of a sudden you're not?"

"Look, it's time we talked. That's all. Are you going to argue with me about it or just let me in?"

She considered it.

"Well?" he asked.

"I'm thinking."

Shaking his head, he snorted. "We can argue later, okay? Let's talk now."

Her eyes narrowed in suspicion. "About what, specifically?"

Instead of answering, he said, "You held your own in the planning meeting today."

That was a lie and she knew it. With so many facts and figures being tossed around, Terri had been too humbled to say much at all. Oh, when asked directly, she'd given her opinion, but that hadn't happened often. Most of the employees were taking their cues from Cooper, and he hadn't exactly been hanging on her every word.

"Not really," she said. "I just didn't stumble on my words."

"It was more than that." He pushed away from the doorjamb. "Have you eaten?"

"Not yet. It's a little early and…"

He looked as irritated as he sounded. And yet, there was something about the energy bristling around him that made him even hotter than before. His jaw was

shadowed with whiskers, those ice-blue eyes were narrowed on her and with that carefully shaggy haircut, he looked like a well-dressed pirate.

With that thought firmly in mind, it didn't take much for Terri's brain to imagine him in tight leather pants, shirtless, swinging a cutlass through the air as he held her pinned tightly to his side. Okay, fine. Maybe she was reading too many romance novels if she was mentally putting Cooper Hayes onto the cover of one.

He snapped his fingers in front of her face and Terri jolted. "Excuse me?"

He shrugged. "You zoned out."

Okay, yes, she had and she didn't want to think about why. "Right. Anyway, it's early. I was going to call room service in a while."

"No need." He held one hand out to her. "Come with me. I want to show you something."

Why was he suddenly paying attention to her? Her mind wanted to know why he'd decided to stop ignoring her existence. What had changed that all of a sudden he was seeking her out? It was a good thing, right? They had to get to know each other. To work together.

But it wasn't work she was thinking about. The gleam in his eyes was a challenge. One she wouldn't turn her back on. Terri put her hand in his and when his fingers closed around hers, she felt a sizzling jolt of electricity that shot up her arm to rattle around in her chest like a crazed ping-pong ball.

He'd felt it, too. She saw a flicker of surprise come

and go from his features—so briefly, maybe no one else would have noticed. But Terri could recognize in him what she was feeling.

Was he fighting it as hard as she was?

Four

Cooper's grip on her hand was gentle, but strong enough to tug her along behind him as he stalked down the hall. She hurried to keep up. "Where are we going?"

"You'll see in a minute."

Back down the elegant hall to the private elevator. "Oh, no, thanks. I just left the offices an hour ago. Not really interested in going back right now."

"We're not going to the office." The doors opened and he tugged her inside. He hit the roof button and Terri's eyes widened.

"The roof?" She looked up at him, confused. "Should I be worried?" she asked, only half joking.

"About what?"

"'Accidentally' falling off?"

Cooper snorted. "I'd never throw you off my own roof. Too obvious."

"Well, I feel better." Since she was watching him, she caught the fleeting smile that was gone almost before it was there.

"You've seen way too many movies."

"I'm not a movie person. I'm a book person."

"You can be both," he pointed out.

"No," she assured him, "you really can't."

"Books, movies, doesn't matter," he said as the elevator stopped. "There are no bad guys here. You don't need to worry. We're not enemies."

Weren't they? Hadn't Dave made a point of letting her know that Cooper wasn't exactly thrilled with having a new partner thrust on him? And really, looking at it from his point of view, why would he be happy about it?

"If we're not enemies, what exactly are we, then?" she asked. She really was interested in what his answer would be.

"That's a good question." Which wasn't an answer at all.

The elevator doors slid open and he stepped outside. He stopped, looked at her and then held out his hand to her again. Silently, he waited and Terri's mind raced. She could refuse. Go back down to her suite and never know why he'd wanted to take her to the roof. She could turn away from this opportunity to talk to him, away from everyone else, to maybe find common ground that could help them both. Or she could fight her fear of heights and go with him.

Not a hard decision at all, because she'd never been one to back away from what scared her. But that wasn't all of it, either. He was so gorgeous, so intense, and when he looked at her, Terri felt heat simmer inside her bones.

She slipped her hand into his and his ice-blue eyes warmed briefly. His fingers closed over hers and her heartbeat galloped in response.

Then she stepped out of the elevator and stopped dead. "Oh, my God."

She let go of his hand, took a deep breath and simply stared. Terri knew Cooper was right behind her, probably watching her reaction, and she didn't care. This was all so…*amazing*. Turning in a slow circle, she tried to take everything in at once. Surprise wasn't a strong enough word for what she was feeling. *Stunned* was pretty close and yet, even that word wasn't enough.

She walked past Cooper, feeling the heat of his body as she brushed against him. It was incredible. She never would have expected to find this in the middle of a desert city. On the roof of a building. But here it was. A fantasy of flowers, potted trees and flowering vines. Polished stones set in patterns along pathways that snaked through the most beautiful garden she'd ever seen.

"This is…wonderful," she whispered almost reverently.

"Yeah, it is." Cooper moved close and stayed at her side as she continued to walk along the smooth stone path. "My dad started it when I was a kid. We lived

here a lot of the time and he wanted me to be able to be outside."

"Seriously?" Well, that piece of information jolted her out of the magic of the place. "He let a *child* come out to the roof?"

He laughed shortly. "If you look close enough, you'll see the Plexiglas barrier. Unless you deliberately try to climb the three feet of concrete and then the five feet of Plexiglas wall, you're not going to fall off."

"Good to know." Still, she deliberately gave the transparent wall—which now that it had been pointed out to her, she could see—a wide berth.

Walking along the polished stone pathway, she followed it through a magical garden with hanging plants, trailing ivy and pots of flowers that tumbled to the ground in brilliant colors.

"When I was a kid, my father had a putting green up here," Cooper mused.

"Really?" She turned her head to look at him, enjoying that he was sharing something of himself. Maybe this was the first step in their getting to know each other.

"Everybody needs a place to relax. This was his." Cooper looked around, taking in the trees, the wooden decking, the raised boxes where chrysanthemums in their brilliant fall colors gave off a spicy scent that flavored the air. "When he died, I kept it all and added to it." He shrugged. "We spent a lot of time together here. I don't come here often now. Not enough time."

"You should make time." She stopped again beside a

pergola with climbing, flowering vines dripping from its roofline like a living curtain.

The scene was set for seduction.

There were chairs, couches, a gas fire pit where flames danced and swayed in the wind sweeping across the roof. A small waterfall tumbled over stones into a weathered brass bowl filled with shining stones, and the splash of the water was as soothing as a touch. But it was the cloth-covered table set with fine china and crystal that drew her attention. It was private. Beautiful.

Romantic.

Seduction.

A ripple of anticipation swirled through her at the thought. She hadn't spent much time with Cooper, but every time she *did* see him, there was a near magnetic attraction that buzzed between them, promising all sorts of…interesting things. Another ripple rolled through her body, and Terri took a shallow breath to steady herself. Really didn't work. How could it? With Cooper standing so close to her, it was a wonder there weren't actual flames licking at her.

She was new here. She was going to be working with this man. Giving into what she was feeling could be a big mistake.

Swallowing hard, she asked, "What's going on?"

Another casual shrug. "An early dinner. We both have to eat. Why not here?"

Because they were alone in the growing darkness but for the twinkling white lights strung through potted trees, flowers and entwined through the vine-covered

pergola roof. It was magical. And here she stood next to Tall, Dark and Tempting. She felt a quick twist of nerves.

Just a few days ago she'd been at home in her own little condo and today she was on top of the world in Las Vegas, about to step into an exciting new life with a man who could start fires in her blood just by looking at her. She'd be weird if she *wasn't* a little nervous.

He tipped his head to one side and studied her. "Problem?"

"No," she said quickly. "No problem."

She might be a little shaky, but she wasn't going to let him see it. He wasn't the first man to give her a look that said he was thinking about devouring her. Of course, he *was* the first man who made her feel the same way in return.

But this wasn't a date. This was dinner with her new business "partner." Though it seemed like he'd gone out of his way to make the setting lush and anything but businesslike. Still, Terri wanted Cooper Hayes to see her not only as desirable, but also as competent and ready for whatever challenges came her way. Nothing wrong with a good facade.

"Good." He held out one hand to her again. "Before dinner arrives, come with me. I want you to see something."

"There's more?" She put her hand in his and told herself to completely disregard that jolt of heat. The cold wind whipping past them didn't stand a chance against the kind of burn he could prompt, and trying to ignore it was a useless endeavor.

His grip on her hand tightened. God, what was it about a strong, quiet man that was so damn sexy? And why couldn't she stop noticing?

Cooper didn't speak, just walked toward the far end of the roof, drawing her with him. As they went, she idly noticed the walkways, the grass, planted in artistic swirls and waves, the fairy lights strung through bushes and plants. There was redwood decking laid out and on it sat a small café table and chairs. It would be a lovely spot to sit and watch the night sky. Then he stopped and she looked up at him. He was staring off into the distance and when Terri turned her head to look, too, her eyebrows rose as she realized they were standing right at the edge of the building.

The only thing between them and a fall to nearly thirty floors below was a thin sheet of Plexiglas tucked into a three foot tall concrete barrier. Instinctively, she tightened her grip on his hand. "Well, this is unsettling."

He laughed shortly. "Still worried about getting tossed off?"

"No." She whipped her hair back out of her face, but the wind simply picked it up and threw it across her eyes again. "And with the way I'm holding on to you, if I go, you're going with me."

He grinned and pulled her close to his side. "Good to know."

"Wow," she said, mesmerized by his amused, unguarded expression. "You should smile more often."

"I'll make a note. So," he asked, "you have a problem with heights, is that it?"

"No," she said, "just a problem with falling."

A short burst of laughter rolled from his chest and settled over her like a warm blanket. Really, Terri knew she was getting pulled deeper and deeper into this attraction she felt for him. That should worry her—and maybe later, she'd take the time to consider it. For right now she decided to enjoy the heat.

"No danger there," he said and his eyes locked with hers. "You won't fall, Terri. But if you did, I'd catch you."

"That shouldn't make me feel better," she admitted, still staring up into eyes that looked both shuttered and open, "but it does."

He smiled at her again, then waved one hand, encompassing the city lights just bursting out of the darkness. "This is what I wanted you to see."

Already the streetlights were blinking on and there were a few headlights shining from the cars streaming down the street. But the real magic slowly began to take shape. Seconds ticked into minutes as they stood there in the growing darkness watching a desert erupt into a neon dream.

As if in a choreographed dance, bright lights decorating the casinos surged into life. Electric signs in every color imaginable lit up the night like an earthbound rainbow and Terri was so fascinated, she forgot all about her fear of falling and took a step closer to the wall.

"It's so beautiful."

"It is," he agreed. "I like standing here at sunset, watching the whole city come to life."

She turned her head to look at him. The wind whipped through his hair and tugged at the edges of his jacket. His gaze held hers and Terri felt that rush of temptation again. He was a man comfortable with his place, sure of himself and who he was, and that was undeniably appealing. His confidence, his surety, was almost palpable and she could see that he would be a formidable enemy.

But wouldn't that also make him an unfaltering friend—or lover?

Deliberately, she turned away from both him and her thoughts and focused on the view. Brilliant lights marched along the Strip like an invading army, lighting up every shadow, outlining every sight in dancing color.

"There's a gigantic Ferris wheel." How had she not noticed it in the daylight?

"It's the High Roller. Caesar's owns it," he said with a touch of pride in his voice he couldn't quite disguise. "Five hundred fifty feet tall."

"I'll take your word for it." She shuddered at the thought of being so high and *moving* at the same time.

"You can see for miles from the top," he said. "It's higher than the London Eye or the Singapore Flyer. Takes a half an hour to make one circle so you can really enjoy the views."

Terri wondered if he realized just how proud he was of his city or how much he loved it. Whenever she'd thought of Las Vegas in the past, it was as a vacation spot. She'd never really considered people who lived

here. Who were a part of this electrified piece of desert. Now she did.

She looked up at his profile as he stared out over the bright lights and thought he looked like an ancient king, standing on the battlements to survey his realm. When he turned his head to meet her gaze, that image remained. He was impossibly good-looking and he wore that aura of strength and power as comfortably as he did the elegantly tailored suit. Cooper Hayes was a nerve-racking man.

Why did she find that so appealing?

Hurriedly, she took a breath and looked toward the lights again. "The Eiffel Tower."

"At the Paris Hotel," he said quietly. "One half scale of the original in France. Have you seen it?"

"No, I've never been out of the country."

"How about New York? The Statue of Liberty here is a one-third scale of the one in New York Harbor."

"I haven't seen that, either."

"You should go. It's damn impressive."

Nodding to herself, she said, "I'll put it on the list."

He chuckled. "You have a list?"

"Of course. The wish list," she said, shifting her gaze to him. "Places I want to see."

"Like…?"

"Oh." She took a breath, thought about it for a minute, then said, "New York, obviously. And I'd like to see the Liberty Bell."

"Really?"

Terri shrugged. "I like history. In fact, there are

lots of places right here in the US I want to visit. But I also want to see Paris, London, Venice, for starters."

"Quite the list."

She tipped her head to one side and studied him. The October wind was cold, but the clear wall in front of them cut most of it. He looked completely at home here on top of the world and she wondered if he'd been *born* with that confidence or if he'd worked to gain it.

"I suppose you've been to all of those places," she said softly.

"And more." He crossed his arms over his chest and stared out at the bright lights. "We've got hotels all over the world, so the business requires me to go."

"You went for *business*?" She shook her head. "That's just sad."

"No, it's not," he argued. "That's life. Work."

"Well, when you see something beautiful, you should take the time to admire it. Enjoy it."

His gaze shifted to hers. "Oh," he said meaningfully, "I am."

Terri swallowed hard against the quickening flames inside her. A single look. A simple sentence. And he turned her inside out.

This was probably not a good sign.

"Well, until you can make that list work for you," he said, the abrupt change in subject making her head swim a bit, "Las Vegas can give you New York, the Eiffel Tower and a trip down the Venice canals."

She smiled, steadier now that she'd had a second to catch her breath. "Plus, no long flights."

"You should do it, you know," Cooper told her. "Take the damn trips. See what you want to see."

"Easy to say," she said, laughing. "But trips cost money and I haven't been able to afford—" Terri broke off because that excuse didn't work anymore. Now she was rich. Rich enough to fly first class. Or maybe charter a jet.

That thought was still mind-boggling.

"Just sinking in, is it?" He nodded thoughtfully. "You can go wherever, whenever you want. Nothing holding you here, is there?"

Interesting way of putting it. "Trying to get rid of me?"

"Oh, if that's what I was doing right now, I'd find a better way."

"Is that right?" She walked with him when he took her arm and steered her back through the garden toward the seating area. "And how would you do it?"

He let go of her arm only to place his hand at the small of her back in a move that was both gentlemanly and enticing. She felt that slight touch as a ribbon of heat across her nerve endings. It was as if there was a live flame against her skin. It was unsettling. And exciting.

Then he spoke. "I could offer to buy you out."

She stopped dead and looked up at him. "Buy me out?"

"Why so offended?" He looked genuinely curious. "It's a hell of an offer and Terri, this isn't your world."

She stiffened a little at the implication. Did he think she *couldn't* fit in, was that it? That was insulting—

although, hadn't she been telling herself the same thing since all of this started? But it was one thing to think it privately and quite another to have someone else point it out. Squaring her shoulders, she stiffened her spine and lifted her chin.

Well, Terri told herself, he was wrong. Was she a little nervous? Sure. But damned if she'd quit just a few days in. "It's my world *now*."

"Is it?" They stood alongside the seating area. Beneath the white twinkling lights, he looked down at her, and his beautiful eyes were in shadow. "Is it really? Or is your life still in Utah? This isn't an adventure, Terri. Not to me. Not to my employees."

"*Our* employees," she corrected and had the satisfaction of seeing him grit his teeth.

"For now, yes. Jacob left you his half of the company, but do you really think he meant for you to do the job? Are you even sure you want to?"

"I won't know until I try, will I?"

A muscle in his jaw twitched. "Hayes Corporation *is* my world and I'll protect it."

"From me?" she asked, all innocence. "Do I look that dangerous to you?"

A slow, tantalizing smile curved one corner of his mouth, and his eyes seemed to darken in the shadows. "Oh, yeah. You're plenty dangerous."

She'd never thought of herself that way, and Terri had to admit that a part of her liked hearing him say it. A swirl of something unexpected rose up from the pit of her stomach, danced around her chest, then reached up and closed her throat. Terri had to force herself to

breathe. She was way out of her depth here. This man was unlike any other she'd ever known and she had the distinct feeling that if she put one foot wrong on this new path she was walking, the fall would feel like she was dropping from the roof of the StarFire.

"My father wanted me here." It felt good to say it aloud. To remind them both that she had a right to be there.

"He did." Cooper nodded. "But I wonder if he wanted you to *stay*."

She didn't know. Had no way of *ever* knowing. But whether Jacob Evans had intended for her to stay in Vegas and make the corporation her life or not, she felt that she owed it to herself to give it a chance. Jan had told her to grab the brass ring and that was just what she was going to do.

"It's my decision, not Jacob's."

"Is it?" he countered. "Or are you thinking you owe something to the father you never knew?"

Heat that had nothing to do with arousal swept through her. "Are you deliberately trying to get me to leave?"

"If I was trying," he said, "you wouldn't know I was trying."

"Well, that's ambiguous enough."

"Just honest," he countered.

"And confusing as well as not very welcoming."

"Blunt again." He smiled. "I like it."

That smile was lethal. Note to self: remember that. He used that oh-so-rare smile like a weapon—to dis-arm and distract. And she couldn't afford to be dis-

tracted. She was going to build a life here and she had to keep on her toes around Cooper Hayes.

As she stood there, Cooper walked to the table, set with fine china, crystal glassware and heavy silver, poured each of them a glass of straw-colored wine, then handed her one of the glasses. Grateful, she took a sip to ease the tightness in her throat. Naturally, it tasted wonderful. She'd already learned that Cooper Hayes did nothing by half measure.

"Look," he said, "we're both in a situation we didn't expect."

"That's fair," she murmured.

That half smile erupted again. "All I'm saying is that we take a few days. See what happens. You learn what you can about the business…"

"What I *can*?" she repeated.

"There's a steep learning curve. No offense intended."

"Hmm." She wasn't sure about that no offense thing. Studying the wine in her glass, she mused, "You know, Utah actually has television now. And the internet. We're still learning how to use it, of course, but we're pretty quick."

His lips twitched and tugged at something inside her. "Point taken. Fine. Sit in on meetings. Ask questions. Get familiar with the place."

"I've talked to a few employees already," she said, accepting his unsaid apology for expecting her to be stupid or something.

"That's not what I meant," Cooper told her. "You

won't learn about the company by talking with random employees."

"You're wrong about that," she said. "Who better to tell me what working here is like? The higher-ups sitting in offices? I don't think so."

Cooper considered that for a second and realized she might be onto something.

"You're...unexpected," he mused.

"What a nice thing to say." She practically beamed at him and Cooper felt the punch of that wide, delighted smile slam into him again.

"Is it?"

"Well, sure." She walked a little closer to the Plexiglas wall, but stopped well clear of it. "I've always done the expected thing, you know? A's in school to please my parents. Business courses in college because it was the right thing to do in spite of my major. My job at the bank. Dating nice, boring guys." She sighed a little. "I'm a rule follower with a rebel soul."

He laughed at that and she gave him a narrow-eyed look over her shoulder. He held up one hand. Couldn't afford to piss her off, could he? He was here to pour on the charm. Making her mad just defeated his whole plan. "Didn't mean to laugh. But if you've got a rebel soul, why don't you let it out once in a while?"

"In a way, I do." She set her wineglass down onto the table. "I say what I think, even when it gets me in trouble."

She intrigued him in spite of how he tried to keep

her at a distance. "If it gets you in trouble, then why do it?"

"Because lies come too easy to people and that's annoying. I'd rather know the truth, hard or not, than some comfortable lie."

"And how's that working for you?"

She actually winced. "Sometimes, not so great. Not that I try to deliberately hurt anyone…"

Yeah, he was getting that. She seemed genuinely concerned with…hell. Everything. So no, if *he* was being brutally honest, he couldn't see her out in a flame war. In his world, lies were the currency of the realm.

Business deals were always smoothed over with exaggeration. Dates were ended with promises of another even when he knew there would never be one. Partnerships were announced when nothing had ever been said about it before. Hadn't Jacob lied to Cooper for years? In *not* telling anyone about the daughter he would leave everything to, he'd lied. He'd let that lie grow. Allowed Cooper to make plans based on the lie.

So maybe she had a point about the power of the truth. Too bad the truth wouldn't help him any.

A bell sounded and Cooper set his wineglass down then strolled to a door behind a huge potted tree. He opened it and a waiter pushing a room service cart came through. "You don't have to serve it, James. We'll take care of that."

"Yes, sir. Good night, sir. Ma'am."

When he was gone, Terri murmured, "I'm not sure I like being a ma'am."

"You don't look like one, if that helps."

She whirled around to meet his gaze and Cooper saw the flash of pleasure in her eyes. He'd like to see more of it.

"What do I look like?"

"Trouble."

She grinned. "Unexpected *and* trouble. Good for me. You know, those short sentences of yours are starting to be appealing."

"Why waste time on words?" he asked, moving in on her.

"No idea," she said, and he swore he could see the pulse point in her neck throbbing.

He hadn't planned to have a taste of her; in fact, he knew the idea could scuttle all his plans, but now that was all he could think of. Here, under the night sky with the city lights glimmering all around them.

"What're you doing?" she asked, her voice a soft hush of sound.

"Thinking about kissing you."

"How much longer are you going to think about it?"

That was all the invitation he needed. He grinned and pulled her in close, threading one hand through her hair to hold her head in place as he closed his mouth over hers. The taste of her seared him. It was more than he'd expected. More than he'd found before with anyone else. Instant heat. Instant need swamping him. He parted her lips, and his tongue swept into her mouth to tangle with hers. She sighed and her breath slid inside him, adding even more intimacy to this stolen moment.

He'd been thinking about her for days. Thinking about doing just this, which is why he'd been avoid-

ing her. Catching glimpses of her in the office or on the casino floor was one thing. Now he had his hands on her at last and he reveled in it.

He slid one hand up beneath the hem of her red silk shirt to cup her breast over the lace of her bra. She trembled and his body responded in a flash. He wanted to feel *her*. Wanted to explore every inch of her and take his time doing it.

She sighed and leaned into him as his thumb stroked across the tip of her nipple. Cooper swallowed a groan and dropped his hand down to her butt, cupping, squeezing, pressing her up against his aching groin.

Deepening the kiss even further, he shifted his hold on her so he could cup her center. She jolted in his arms and instinctively spread her legs farther apart. It was good, but it wasn't enough. Not nearly. He needed to touch her. *Now.*

"Don't let me interrupt." A voice sounded out from somewhere behind them. "No, wait. Yes, let me interrupt."

Five

Cooper broke the kiss and rested his forehead against Terri's. Dammit. He knew that voice. He hadn't heard it in almost two years, but he wasn't likely to forget it. "Celeste."

Terri looked past his shoulder and her mouth dropped open. "You're *Vega*."

Cooper turned in time to see Celeste Vega's gorgeous features brighten into a pleased smile.

"Ah, you know me. Isn't that lovely?" She stalked toward them, slid the gold chain of her bag off her shoulder and dropped it onto a chair. Picking up Cooper's wineglass, she took a long drink and smiled at Terri again. "Yes, I am Vega. I always loved to come to Las Vegas. The headlines would read, *Vega in Vegas*. Such symmetry," she cooed.

Cooper buried the groan building in his chest. His body ached, his temper was quickly on the rise and he was fresh out of patience for his former lover. "What're you doing here, Celeste?"

Rather than answer, she finished off his wine, handed him the empty glass and said, "I wanted to see you, of course. And how delicious that I find you here, on the roof, where we share so many lovely memories."

Cooper felt Terri stiffen beside him and he could have cheerfully tossed Celeste out of his hotel on her beautiful ass.

Reluctantly, Cooper gave the intruder his full attention because anything less would be dangerous. She was still beautiful. Celeste Vega's striking face had graced the covers of hundreds of magazines. She'd walked the runways in Paris and New York and remained the toast of Europe.

Almost six feet tall, Celeste had short, dark brown hair, shot through with strands of gold and red, cut into a style that hugged her jawline. Her caramel-colored skin seemed to glow against the white silk shirt and slacks she wore. Her almond-shaped, golden-brown eyes could tempt a man into just about anything and in the past, her sultry gaze had worked on him. But as he still had the taste of Terri in his mouth and the memory of her lush body pressed against his fresh in his mind, Celeste's surprise arrival did nothing for him.

Besides, why would he be glad to see her? Nearly two years ago, Celeste had walked out on him in favor of a much older man with a title and a few billion more than Cooper.

"Again. What're you doing here, Celeste?"

She pouted. It was an expression meant to seduce and it had actually worked on him, once upon a time. He was wiser now.

"Why, I almost feel that you're not happy to see me," she said, pout still in place.

"And how did you get up to the roof?" he demanded.

"Ah, one of your lovely minions opened the elevator to me and before you ask, no, I won't tell you who. You would no doubt torture them for their kindness." Brushing past him, one hand to his chest, she continued, "Cooper, introduce me to your new playmate."

"I'm Terri. Terri Ferguson." She held out one hand that Celeste ignored in favor of air kissing both of Terri's cheeks.

"Well, aren't you adorable? I can see why our Cooper was so eager to get you on the rooftop for one of his famous private dinners." She tossed a sly smile at Cooper, then dropped one arm around Terri's shoulders and steered her toward the table where dinner waited. "Oh. Dinner for two. We'll share, yes?"

Cooper swallowed back the rush of irritation that was nearly choking him. But on the other hand, maybe it was a good thing she'd crashed the party. She'd kept him from going too far too fast with Terri. Celeste was a force of nature. There was no point in trying to get rid of her. She wouldn't go, short of having security escort her out.

She was beautiful and treacherous and Cooper wondered what the hell she was up to.

The following morning Terri sat at her birth father's desk and looked at the stacks of files piled up in front

of her. She'd asked for information on the Hayes hotels and now she had enough reading material to last her a year. But to understand this company, she had to immerse herself in it.

She still felt like an impostor. Even more so now, after meeting Celeste Vega the night before. Clearly, the world-famous model and Cooper had had a relationship. And just as clearly, he wasn't happy that the woman had dropped in on him.

Famous rooftop dinners.

Those words echoed in Terri's mind. Last night she'd thought he'd done something special. Just for her. Was she really no more than one more link in a chain of Cooper's women? But as soon as she thought it, she let it go. She *wasn't* one of his women. She was half-owner of this hotel—this corporation. Whatever else went on between her and Cooper, that one fact wouldn't change.

One kiss was hardly a relationship. Though granted, that one kiss was pretty spectacular.

She shivered just remembering the feel of his mouth on hers. Of his hands sweeping up and down her body, the breath-stealing, soul-shaking response that had clattered through her.

Yeah. Okay. Maybe it wasn't a relationship, but it was definitely *something*. But a better question would be: Did she *want* more from Cooper than simple respect and acceptance of her right to be there? She didn't know. Oh, her body knew exactly what it wanted, but that didn't mean it was going to get it.

"Doesn't matter," Terri murmured, while her mind

ran an obstacle course of scattered thoughts. "I'm here now. That's what matters."

Sitting in her birth father's office she tried not to feel intimidated by what Jacob had left her. That was a useless endeavor, though. Beyond the closed door of *her* office, people were busy, running the company she'd stumbled into. And she...was trying to catch up.

Resolute, she snatched the top folder off the stack and looked at the photo on the front. *Hayes London*. The hotel looked like a small castle and she had no doubt at all that on the inside, it was a true palace. As good a place as any to start, she told herself.

Then her phone rang, signaling a video chat, and Terri reached for it like it was a rope tossed to her in a raging river. As soon as she answered, Terri smiled. "Hi, Mom."

"Hi, baby girl." Carol Ferguson looked great. At sixty-five, she was fit and pretty with short, stylish blond hair that would never give in to gray. "How's it going?"

"I don't know." Terri held her phone and sat back in her chair. "How's Daisy?"

"Really?" Carol asked, both eyebrows rising high on her forehead. "You want to talk about your dog?" She shrugged. "Okay, we'll start there. Daisy's great. She's taken over the couch completely, bullied the neighbor's beagle, dug up your aunt Connie's tulip bulbs and is, right now, snoring." She turned the phone so that Terri could see her adorable mutt spread-eagled on her mom's brown leather couch.

"So, now that you know Daisy's fine, how about you tell me how you are?"

"First," Terri said, wincing a little, "tell Aunt Connie I'm sorry about the bulbs."

Her mother waved her hand. "Don't worry about it. Connie can't grow weeds. Those bulbs never would have bloomed. She'll do what she always does. Buy plants in pots, bury the pots and then take credit for growing the flowers."

Terri laughed, delighted at the description because it really was *so* Connie. And wow, it felt good to relax and laugh with someone who loved her. Who understood what she was going through.

"Now, talk to me, sweetie." Her mom's face held the I'm-not-taking-no-for-an-answer expression Terri was all too familiar with.

"Okay, then. This hotel is amazing," she said and chuckled at the use of that word again. Seriously, she was going to have to buy a thesaurus or something. "Mostly, everyone's been very nice. I'm staying in Jacob's suite at the very top of the hotel and—"

"Ouch." Her mom winced. "Too bad they didn't have suites on the ground floor for you."

She grinned. It was good to have people who knew you that well. "I'm dealing. I even went out on the roof last night with Cooper."

"Is that right?" Carol made a *hmmmm* of interest. "Cooper, huh? Is he as pretty in person?"

"Prettier, though he wouldn't love that description."

"Men so rarely do. On the roof? Why?"

Well, now, that was the question, wasn't it? She'd

thought it was to share the view. And a romantic dinner. Now she wondered. "He wanted to show me the view and it's beautiful, if scary, to be looking down from about a million feet in the air."

"Uh-huh. Anything else?"

"Well, Celeste Vega showed up."

"*The* Vega?" Her mom's eyebrows rose even higher. Not surprising. Terri's mother was practically addicted to those magazines at checkout counters. She bought them every week and was up-to-date on all the celebrities. She could tell you who was married, getting divorced, going into rehab. Her celebrity love was wide and vast. "Is she as beautiful in person or is it all airbrushing? I've wondered about that. You know you can't trust pictures. These days they could make a troll look like a beauty queen."

Terri laughed. "She's definitely not a troll. Actually, she's even more beautiful in real life. Tall, elegant. Intimidating."

"Why?" Carol argued. "You're very pretty yourself."

"Thanks, *Mom*. No bias there." Still smiling, Terri continued. "She seems very nice…" Her voice trailed off.

"I hear a *but* coming…?"

"But nothing, really." Terri recovered quickly. She didn't want to tell her mother about the romance of the night that Cooper had arranged. About the kiss, about Vega's interruption and then finding out that Terri had only been one of a crowd of women who'd been given that "special" night.

She flipped open the folder in front of her and idly glanced at the photos of the interior of the London

Hayes hotel. Just as she'd assumed. Gorgeous. Old world elegance. Sighing, she said, "I'm trying to find my feet here, Mom, but honestly, I'm a little lost, still. I'm going to make this work, though. This is an incredible chance for me, so I'll figure it out."

"Why isn't your new partner helping you?" Carol's eyes flashed and her mouth turned down into what Terri recognized as her going into battle scowl.

"He's a little busy, running the whole company." Terri got up out of the desk chair, walked to the couch and sat down again, curling her legs beneath her. Across the room there were wide windows giving her an extensive view of a bright blue desert sky.

"Cooper's got his hands on everything. He's running this whole company. He can't really hold my hand and walk me through all of this." All true, but what she wasn't adding was that Cooper didn't seem to really *want* her to succeed. Oh, he'd never come right out and said it, but he'd made it plain he'd be fine with it if she gave up and went away. And that would be easier, she told herself.

But she wasn't going to quit. There was a beautiful door open for her and she planned on walking through it.

Taking a breath, she said, "His assistant, Dave Carey, has been helpful, though. He's the one who showed me around the offices, and he's offered to help any way he can."

"I suppose that's fine, then. At least someone there is helping you. But if everything's going so nicely, why aren't you happy?" Before Terri could speak, her

mother said, "Don't bother denying it. I can see it on your face. You're feeling out of place and useless."

Terri laughed and pushed one hand through her hair. "Are you psychic?"

"No, just your mother." Carol turned her head and shouted, "I'll be there in a minute, Connie!" Shaking her head, she looked at Terri again. "Sorry, sweetie. Your aunt Connie and I are off to play tennis with some friends in a minute and you know how crazed my sister is about punctuality."

Good to know that at least *one* of them had their life in order, Terri thought. "I'm not sure what to do here, Mom."

"Well, of course you don't. You haven't even been there a week. Give yourself a chance, honey."

A chance. But only last night Cooper had pretty much told her that trying was a waste of time. That she couldn't do it. But that just meant he didn't know her very well. Terri could do it. Her father had left it to her. Her Dad had taught her to believe in herself and her Mom had taught her to dream. No way was she backing out.

"You're thinking too much," her mother said with a dramatic sigh. "You always do this. You question, rethink and reevaluate way too much. Feel your way through instead. You have good instincts, sweetie. Trust them. You're smart. Capable." She took a breath and huffed it out. "What was it your dad used to say to you all the time?"

A reluctant smile curved Terri's mouth as she re-

membered. She lowered her voice in imitation and said, "Terri, honey, there is *nothing* you can't do."

"Exactly." Her mother nodded sharply. "Now, stop doubting yourself and get out there and show them what a Ferguson can do when she makes up her mind."

Her mom had a point. She was sitting here going over and over everything she'd said and done in the past few days and getting exactly nowhere. Time to jump in with both feet, so to speak. "Okay, Mom, I will."

"I'm going to say it again, just for emphasis. Feel your way through, Terri. Go with your gut. It's a good one. Trust it."

A wave of affection rolled over her as she smiled at the woman who had raised her, loved her and taught her to stand up for herself. "I really love you."

"Of course you do!" Carol blew her a kiss. "I love you, too. Oh, for God's sake, now your aunt Connie's in the driveway honking the horn. The neighbors are going to have a fit."

Terri laughed. "You'd better go, Mom. And thanks. For everything."

"Love you!"

Once she hung up, Terri walked back to the desk, sat down and picked up the London hotel folder. The pictures were beautiful and reports from hotel managers would be informative. But she really wanted to know what their *guests* had to say about their stays at a Hayes hotel.

She dropped the folder and booted up the computer on her desk instead. She'd learn everything she could

about the Hayes Corporation. She'd read customer reviews, check out travel bloggers and— "Oh, no."

Headlines covered the web browser page and right at the top she read *Shakeup at Hayes Corporation— Jacob Evans's daughter to take over half the company. How will this affect stock prices? Does Cooper Hayes know how to share?*

"Oh, God." She scanned the brief article, wondering what her mom and everyone she knew would think about it. Her mind raced even as her mother's advice echoed in the back of her brain.

And of course there were pictures along with the article. Cooper looked fantastic of course—all steely-eyed and tough in a zillion-dollar suit. But it looked as though they'd dug up a picture of Terri from her college years. She was wearing holey jeans, her hair was pulled into a ponytail jutting from the side of her head and the guy beside her—Tom? Micah?—was wearing a kilt.

"Very nice," she murmured, sinking back into her chair. Great. Even the media doesn't think she can do this But, look how surprised everyone will be when she did. "Upside? At least only a few million people will see it."

Dave looked up at the woman in his office and knew he'd done the right thing in calling her. With Celeste Vega around, no heterosexual male would be able to think of anyone else.

"She's nothing," Celeste said, walking the perimeter of Dave's office like an exotic cat. "I don't know

why you were worried. She's boring and her breasts are too big."

Personally, Dave thought Terri had a great body, but that wasn't what Celeste wanted to hear. Like most incredibly beautiful women, she preferred thinking that only *she* could snag a man's attention. And to be honest, he reminded himself, that was usually true. In fact, just looking at Celeste from across the room had Dave's pulse pounding. Hell, he was no more immune than any other man when it came to this stunning woman.

When Celeste Vega walked into a room, every other female there seemed to fade into the background. Usually. Once upon a time, Cooper had been completely under her spell. All Dave had to do was arrange for that to happen again.

"Terri's large breasts don't seem to matter to Cooper," Dave pointed out and had the satisfaction of seeing a snap of temper spark in those golden eyes. Good. Even if she didn't actually *want* Cooper back, her ego would never allow her to lose to another woman.

Celeste took a deep breath, then released it slowly as she nodded. "That's because I hurt him terribly when I walked away from him. He must have been bereft."

Dave looked down so he could roll his eyes without being spotted. Celeste might have hurt Cooper but he hadn't exactly locked himself away to recover. Instead, he'd screwed half of Vegas. But whatever.

"I'm sure that's it," Dave soothed. "The point is, we need him to stop wanting Terri long enough that he'll remember she doesn't belong here."

She waved one hand and sunlight flashed off the

gold bangles on her wrist, nearly blinding Dave. "Please. I've come back. Cooper won't be interested in her much longer."

"You might have to work at it, Celeste." Dave leaned back in his chair, propped one foot on his knee and folded his hands over his abdomen. "He's not really fond of you, and Terri's got his attention now."

"It's her homebody appeal, I think," she mused, unbuttoning one of the buttons on the forest green silk shirt she wore. It hung partially off her shoulders and with yet another button undone, gave a tantalizing glimpse of golden-brown skin.

"Do you know up on the roof last night, she was wearing plain black cotton slacks? Can you imagine?" She shook her head as if still stunned. *"Cotton."*

From what Dave had seen, Cooper didn't much care what Terri was wearing. He seemed to be more interested in getting her out of her clothes altogether.

Celeste set both hands at her hips. "She's different, that's all. And I can fix that."

Intrigued, Dave asked, "How?"

"How *all* of life's problems are solved, David. Shopping." She smiled to herself and it was so cat-like, Dave thought she might purr. "I'll take her to the Venetian's shops. We'll deck her out in silks and then Cooper will see that she *still* doesn't fit in."

"What?" That made zero sense.

She sighed. "Right now he's overlooking how unsuitable she is, because she's dressed like a farm girl. So he gives her the benefit of the doubt. But once she has appropriate clothing, he'll see that the farm girl is

still there. Don't you understand? He excuses the way she doesn't belong because she doesn't look as though she should. But once she's dressed properly, Cooper will acknowledge that she'll never fit into his world."

"Sounds convoluted to me." Shaking his head, he pointed out, "Making her even more attractive isn't going to make him *stop* wanting her."

"Nothing will," she said. "Until he's ready. Right now she's new. She's a fascination. Even though he knows he doesn't want her here, in the company, he wants her in his bed."

"Yeah. I know. That's the problem."

"No, that's the solution. If they have sex, all the better for us."

"What the hell are you talking about?"

"It's sad, really," she said with a dramatic sigh. "You men think sex solves everything. A woman can tell you that sex only creates different problems."

"How's that?" He was not convinced.

"Cooper doesn't want a partner. But he wants *her*." She frowned at that admission. "Once he has her, he has new problems. She'll dig in. Get stars in her eyes. And that will be enough to convince Cooper to send her packing."

Dave stood up, pushed the edges of his jacket back and stuffed his hands into his pockets. He hated to admit it, but she had a point. "You might be onto something."

"*Might be?*" Celeste laughed shortly. "Trust me, David. If there is one thing I know, it's *men*."

She stopped walking, set both hands at her hips

and gave him a glare that should have coated his body in ice. "You called me here to help you get rid of her, right?"

"Yes." No matter what, they had to get rid of Terri.

"Then you should probably leave it to me."

He shook his head. "This is too important, Celeste. For both of us. Your old Count Whoever died before he could marry you and you want Cooper back. I want Terri out of here so I can get the reward I was promised for more than a damn decade. So if you think I'm going to take a step back and give you carte blanche, you're out of your damn mind."

"Fine." She inhaled sharply. "But stay out of my way, David, or I'll let Cooper know what you're up to."

"That's not a smart play, Celeste, and no matter what, you've always been smart."

"So true." She smiled at him and Dave felt a slam of pure appreciation hit him. "Very well. We're on the same side in this."

Partners. Just like Cooper and Terri.

And with any luck, neither partnership would last very long.

Six

The following day Terri sat in on a meeting and listened to everyone talking. This was the second time she'd attended one of these summits and she was feeling a little better than she had the first time. Maybe it was the pep talk from her mother, or maybe it was simply that she was getting used to the idea of her new life. But either way, Terri was determined to have her say this time. She had an idea that she was sure was a good one and whatever it took, she would be heard.

Ten people sat around a conference table, with Cooper at one end and Terri at the other. She caught him looking at her more than once, but then he would turn that icy focus on one of the others and she could breathe again. Even in a business situation, Cooper stirred something inside her that wouldn't be ignored.

He was obviously the king of the room, with the men and women gathered around the table all jostling for his attention.

With all of the opinions being argued, voices raised to talk over each other, Terri tried to follow it all. But more important, she waited for her chance to speak up herself. This was her chance to get not only Cooper's attention, but everyone else's, as well. She'd looked through a lot of the specs on the Hayes hotels all over the world and she knew that expansion was in the works again.

While most of the members of the board were interested in going into new, untested markets, Cooper wanted more than one Hayes hotel in the major cities where they were already a force to be reckoned with. She could see both points of view, but her idea might bridge them. She hadn't heard anyone else bring up what she was thinking, but for all she knew this idea had been discussed and dismissed in some earlier meeting. So she was taking a risk, but if she was going to make this her new life, then she had to step up and take a stand.

She tapped her fingers against the cover of the file on the Hayes London hotel. She'd gone over it, front to back. Terri knew it was a five-star—she'd expected nothing less—and that the hotel restaurant had two Michelin stars. She knew it was in the center of Hyde Park and that the rich and famous regularly stayed there. What she didn't know was why Hayes Corporation needed *another* five-star hotel in the same city.

"I'm saying simply that moving the corporation into

an area completely lacking in five-star accommodation puts us at the top of the mountain." A gray-haired man in a black suit fixed his gaze on the woman in a cherry-red suit sitting opposite him.

This would be so much easier on her, Terri thought, if she could remember their names. But there were so many of them and she hadn't been there very long.

"My point, that you seem to overlook time and again," the woman said, "is that if there are no five-star resorts in those areas, then there may be a reason for that."

"*May* be?" he countered. "What kind of research did you have to do to come up with that?"

"My research is impeccable as always," the woman retorted. "When the wealthy go off to play, they expect more than a view to entertain them. And most of these locations you're suggesting are so isolated, we might as well build a five-star monastery."

That statement got everyone talking. Agreement, argument, voices erupted around the table and Cooper caught Terri's gaze. He looked irritated and almost out of patience.

This was a perfect time for her to speak up.

"Excuse me." When no one quieted, she said it again, louder. "Excuse me."

Her insides were jumping but her voice was steady as she met the eyes of everyone who turned to look at her in turn. They were all surprised, as if a kitten had suddenly morphed into a tiger. Well, Terri couldn't blame them for that, could she? The few times she'd

met them, she'd been too nervous to talk at all. Too convinced she didn't have the right to an opinion.

But her mom had been correct. And her dad's advice echoed in her mind. *There's nothing you can't do.*

Today she was going to prove him right.

"You have something to add, Terri?" Cooper's gaze locked on her. She read neither encouragement nor condemnation on his face and realized she didn't need either one to make her point.

"Actually, yes," she said, "I do."

A couple of the older men sighed audibly and fell back in their leather chairs as if they'd been shot. Even the women didn't look happy to hear from her. No doubt because they'd had to work for years to earn a spot at this table and Terri had simply been born into it. Well, that wasn't her fault, was it? She hadn't asked for any of this, but now that it was here, she wouldn't run from it, either. At least, not without trying to make it work.

"I was looking at the Hayes London—"

"We're talking about a location in Prague," the older man in black said, not bothering to hide his impatience.

"I realize that." Terri nodded, ignoring his rudeness.

"We don't need a hotel in Prague and we've already got one in London," the blonde in red announced.

A rumble of voices began and Terri knew she would lose them all if she didn't speak up fast. It seemed she would have to fight to be heard. Well, she was ready.

"I'm talking about London," she said, loud enough that she commanded everyone's attention. "I agree that we should have a second hotel there—"

"Of course you do," the older man said with a snort of derision. "You're going to agree with Cooper because you're new here and you want to show him he can count on your vote."

"Eli…" Cooper's voice was a low-pitched warning.

The man disregarded it and slapped one hand against the table. "Cooper, we've been over this already and—"

"If you'd let me finish," Terri interrupted. Eli looked at her, stunned that she would so effortlessly put him in his place. When he was quiet again, she said, "Thank you."

Shifting her gaze to Cooper, she saw a flicker of admiration in his eyes. But she couldn't think about that at the moment. Instead, she focused on the notes she'd brought with her to the meeting.

"In looking at some of our top hotels—" Yes, she'd said *our* and that was a stretch for her. But Terri thought it was important to remind everyone here that whether they approved or not, she was a full partner in the Hayes Corporation.

While she had their attention, she continued. "The main thing I noticed was that the hotels are exclusive to the point that ordinary mortals could never afford to stay there."

The blonde in red gave a dramatic sigh and tapped her long, red nails against the table top. "That is rather the point of a five-star luxury getaway."

"Agreed." Terri barely looked at her, thus dismissing her. "And my point is that we're cutting ourselves off from most of the population."

"And your suggestion is, to what," another man far-

ther down the table asked, "hold a half-off sale every other week?"

Cooper's features remained blank. He remained silent. And Terri knew it was because he was waiting to see how she'd handle herself.

"No, that's not the idea," Terri said, giving the rude man a bright smile just to make him feel lousy. "But we'll save that for later, okay?" Looking from face to face, she said, "My idea is to build a second Hayes Hotel in London—as a test case of sorts. We can call it Hayes 2. With a stylized number two to differentiate between this one and the five-star."

"To what purpose?" Eli asked with a sigh.

"Affordable luxury," Terri said and every head in the room turned to look at her. She wasn't cowed. "We offer this affordable luxury to families. To honeymooners. To seniors off exploring the world."

A few mutters, but no one stopped her. Success of a sort, Terri decided, and kept going.

"At Hayes 2, we still give the A-plus service we're known for, but we also make it family friendly." She took a breath. "At the London hotel, we could work with the tourism industry already there. With every visit we can offer double-decker tours of London in the famous red buses. Or half off tickets on the London Eye—"

A couple of people were watching her with interest now and Terri deliberately avoided looking at Cooper. She didn't want to know what he thought of any of this before she'd had time to finish.

"We're not known for family vacations," Eli said tightly.

"Doesn't mean we can't be," Terri told him, then shifted her gaze around the table, avoiding Cooper. Some of them looked interested; others not so much. But she hadn't lost them completely. And now that she was talking about her idea, she warmed to it and her voice and body language helped sell it.

"If we offer families a safe, beautiful place to stay, they'll come. The adults will get that taste of luxury, but in a safe place that welcomes their children. Seniors would enjoy a plush vacation site without draining their retirement accounts. And if London works out, and I think it will, we can do this all over the world."

She splayed her hands on the folder in front of her. "Everywhere there's a Hayes hotel, we build a Hayes 2. We become the premium place to stay for everyone, not just the uber-wealthy."

Silence. That could be good. Or bad. It was hard to tell, just looking at the faces around her, what they were thinking. But no one had shrieked *that's ridiculous* and stomped off.

That had to be a plus.

"We've never considered this before," Eli mused, tapping his index finger against his upper lip.

"Maybe we should have." Cooper spoke up and instantly, everyone's attention was on him. "It's an interesting idea," he continued. "We'll need some hard numbers, though. I want to know just how many families vacation together in big cities. What they do, how much they spend." He swiveled his head and pinned a

man in his forties. "Ethan, get me as much as you can by tomorrow."

"On it."

"I want location suggestions. In London." He gave the blonde in red a nod. "Sharon, you're on that."

"By tomorrow," she promised.

"And we meet again tomorrow afternoon to discuss the findings. Three o'clock here."

Murmurs of agreement blended with the soft scrape of chair legs against carpeted floors. Cooper kept his gaze locked with Terri's as everyone else filed out of the meeting room.

"You surprise me."

"Good. That's almost as nice to hear as 'unexpected' and 'honest.'"

He snorted, shook his head and leaned back in the black leather chair. "How'd you come up with this family thing?"

She tipped her head to one side and looked at him for a long second or two. "In the real world, 'family' isn't a 'thing.' It just is."

"Uh-huh." His gaze pinned her. "So what made you come up with it?"

Sighing a little, she stood up, walked to the end of the table and took a seat beside him. "You know I've been wandering through the hotel, looking around, talking to people."

He nodded.

"Well, I was at the pool, talking to Travis the lifeguard—"

"The lifeguard."

"That's right. Anyway, he was saying how the pool was rarely busy because the guests don't really want to get their hair wet or something—" What she didn't say was, she'd seen it for herself. Yes, October was cool, even in the desert, but warm enough for the "beautiful people" to stretch out on chaises beside the pool. When she was there, a sole man had been swimming laps.

"Travis has a lot to say…"

"Don't get all huffy," she said quickly. "I asked him."

He frowned. "What the hell is huffy? Never mind. Go on."

"Anyway, there are some kids here, but the pool's so deep it's really not child friendly."

"We have a kid's pool," he argued.

"Please." Shaking her head sadly, she said, "It's like the size of a hot tub. Kids need room to play. With slides and water toys and—"

He held up one hand. "I get it. So from this, you decided we should go into the family hotel business?"

Terri shrugged. "I'm from Utah. People there have lots of kids. And they take vacations. People with kids like nice hotels, too. But if the kids are bored, no fun for anyone."

"I didn't say it was a bad idea."

"You didn't say it was a good one, either."

"Does it matter to you what I think of it?"

"Well, yes." She leaned back in the chair and slowly swiveled it back and forth. "We're partners, right?"

He studied her and those cool-as-ice eyes gave nothing away. All Terri knew for sure was that she'd survived the meeting, and that Cooper was still making

her feel things she probably shouldn't. But oh, the burn and sizzle in her blood felt good anyway. And on that score…she needed to know something. "Vega seems nice."

He snorted, pushed out of his chair and walked across the room to the small refrigerator installed in a wet bar/coffee station. "No. Celeste is many things but I wouldn't say 'nice' was in the mix."

"She's beautiful." Terri watched him and her gaze dropped unerringly to his butt. A really excellent behind.

"Absolutely."

"You know her well?" *None of your business, Terri.* But she couldn't help herself.

He glanced at her over his shoulder. "Are you asking if we're lovers?"

Well, she preferred *blunt.* "I guess I am."

"We used to be. Now we're not."

"Okay. Good to know." *Really good.* Because there was just no way Terri Ferguson from Ogden, Utah, could compete with Celeste Vega, supermodel. Not that a single kiss meant that anything was going on between them. Although the fact that she wanted more than that one kiss might. But the point was, Celeste Vega was out of the picture.

Okay, back to what they'd been talking about. "So did you think it was a good idea or not?"

"It's interesting," he allowed thoughtfully. "We've never focused on families as guests."

"I know. I looked at about a hundred of the files." She stood up and walked around the corner of the table.

"Hayes Paris is lovely. Really. But if you had a Hayes 2 there, you could tie it in with Paris Disney. Give the families that visit a real experience. And gondola rides in Venice and skiing lessons in Switzerland and—" His mouth tightened. "You hate it."

"No. I don't."

"And yet, you don't look happy about it."

"I'm not a big smiler, in case you hadn't noticed."

"Why not? You should be happy."

"Is that right?" He tipped his head to one side and gave her a cool stare that didn't even slow her down.

"Well, yeah. You're a bazillionaire, you're gorgeous, you live on top of a palace, probably have hot and cold running women. Why aren't you happy?"

If anything, his frown deepened, so maybe she'd struck a nerve. And she wasn't sure how she felt about that.

"I don't have hot and cold running women," he muttered.

She was glad to hear it. "Okay…but the rest is true."

"Is there a reason why you're concerned about my level of happiness?"

"I'm a humanitarian?"

His lips twitched briefly. "Yeah, that must be it."

The conversation had shifted from business to personal and Terri knew she shouldn't, but she wanted more. "When did you lose your father?"

He blinked. "Well, that came out of left field."

"I'm sorry." She pushed her hair back from her face. "I don't even know why I asked that. But I've been

thinking a lot lately about fathers—my dad and Jacob Evans. So I was wondering about your father."

He nodded and bent down to open the fridge. After another second or two of admiring his behind, Terri deliberately shifted her gaze to avoid the chance of drooling. So instead, she looked around the room. As meeting rooms went, it was, of course, palatial. With gray walls, navy blue trim and a table big enough to comfortably sit twenty people.

When Cooper stood up again, he was holding two water bottles. He carried them back and handed one to her. Twisting the cap off his, he said, "My dad died ten years ago."

"I'm sorry."

"Yeah, me, too." He looked up to a row of pictures on the wall opposite them. "My dad bought this hotel forty years ago."

"Really?" She took a sip of her water and set it down just before Cooper took her hand and led her close to the framed black-and-white photos.

"There it is. Or was," Cooper amended wryly. "The StarFire. Six floors of average rooms and a casino the size of my living room." He smiled looking at the photo and Terri studied it with him.

In the grainy image she saw a man in his thirties, hands in his pockets, grinning at the photographer with a look of pride on his face. The hotel was nothing like its current incarnation. There was no dancing fountain out front to dazzle tourists. No wide, fancy entry-way hustling with bellhops. But, looking at Cooper's

father, she could see the promise of what would come shining in his eyes.

"A year after he bought it, Dad was deep into remodeling—" He paused. "Not into *this*, but updating, improving the casino. Anyway, he needed an investor. Jacob had money and wanted in on the ground floor. So he and Dad became partners in Hayes Corporation and the rest is history, I guess."

"It's come a long way."

"Really has," he agreed. "And now we're worldwide. At least Dad lived long enough to see that happen."

She turned her head to look at his profile as he stared at his father's picture. "You miss him."

"Every damn day." His voice was low and filled with more emotion than Terri had ever heard from him.

She gave his hand a squeeze in solidarity. "I know just how that feels. My dad was smart and wickedly funny and sometimes I ache to hear his voice again. To hear 'Hi, Princess,' when I call. To get a hug. To hear him laugh."

Cooper looked down at her as his grip on her hand tightened. For a second or two they simply stared at each other. Survivors of a loss that still haunted each of them.

"My dad would have liked you," Cooper finally said.

"Why?"

"Because you don't play games. There's no BS with you and that's what he was like, too."

Terri smiled. "You keep complimenting me."

He grinned briefly. "I don't know that most women would call that a compliment."

"I do."

"I know you do," he murmured, staring down into her eyes. "I'm trying to sort that out."

Terri smiled up at him. "Are you saying I'm not only unexpected, but a mystery?"

One corner of his mouth tilted up. "I suppose I am."

"What a nice thing to say." Terri felt that flutter of something warm and oh so nice fill her chest. He not only looked great, he smelled wonderful. And the longer she stood here next to him, the more of a temptation he became.

He admitted quietly, "You're making me think things I shouldn't."

"Why shouldn't you?"

"It would make things even more complicated than they already are."

"And we don't need more complications," she finished for him.

"Might be worth it, though," he mused, tugging her a little closer.

"We should probably find out," Terri said, moving into his arms, tipping her face up to his.

"Research, research," he muttered and smiled briefly before claiming her mouth in a kiss that was instantly soul-searing.

Terri wrapped her arms around his neck and held on tightly as his tongue tangled with hers. Every cell in her body was putting on a party hat and hanging streamers. Her stomach did a wild spin and tumble and it felt as though her blood was heating, thickening in

her veins. Complications be damned. Her mind shut down and her body happily took over.

His hands roamed up and down her back and Terri loved the rush of warmth that he left in his wake. Then she was grateful—grateful that she'd worn a simple yellow dress with a full skirt and a tight waist. Cooper swept the hem of her skirt up and then slid his hand beneath the thin elastic band of her lace panties.

She tore her mouth from his and her head fell back as he cupped the center of her, stroking that one *wonderful* spot where sensations gathered expectantly. Again and again, his thumb moved over that hard, tight spot and she trembled in response. She held on to him as she rode the waves of what he was making her feel. He dropped his head to kiss her neck, the line of her throat, the tip of his tongue stroking her skin.

"Cooper…"

"Come," he whispered against her throat as he pushed her higher, both of them breathing hard and fast. "Just let go, Terri."

A moment later she did. She couldn't have stopped the flash of release even if she'd tried. Her body quaked helplessly; her hips rocked into his hand and her fingers dug into his shoulder as she looked for purchase in a suddenly spinning world.

The climax seemed to roll on and on and Cooper kept it going, his fingers, pushing her along, not giving her time to breathe as jolt after jolt rippled through her until she finally slumped bonelessly against him.

He pulled his hand free, smoothed her skirt back into place, then cradled her tightly to him, lowering

his face to hers for another kiss. This one was as hungry as the last, telling Terri that what was simmering between them was far from over.

"Okay," she whispered at last, "that was…worth a complication or two."

"Good," he said. "Because I've got more complications in mind."

She looked up at him and saw the need flashing in his eyes. Saw the tightness in his jaw and felt tension radiating from his body. She felt it, too. Now that she'd had a small sample of what he could do to her with a touch, she wanted more.

The ornate clock hanging on the far wall began to chime softly and Terri gasped. "I have to go."

Wryly, he said, "Not the reaction I was hoping for."

"No." She laughed, smoothed her hair and tried to ignore the fact that her body was still humming. "Would you ask someone to put those files I brought with me back in my office?" *My* office. Funny how naturally that had come out. She picked up her bottle of water and took a long drink. Wow. Orgasms—and irresistible men—could really make your throat dry. "I'd do it, but I don't want to be late."

"Sure. And late where?"

"I told Debra down at reception that I would be there at two." Terri moved for the door quickly. "She's going to show me around, walk me through the reservation process."

"Why?"

She stopped. "Why what?"

"Why do you need to know how reservations work?"

"Well, if I'm going to do this, I want to learn as much as I can." She threw a quick look at the clock again. "Really have to go. Bye."

She stopped when he called her name. Looking back at him from the door, she waited.

"Dinner tonight. At the Sky restaurant. Then we'll take in Darci Ryan's show in the Shooting Star amphitheater."

Her heart jumped. "That sounds suspiciously like a date. What about complications?"

"Think we've already proven we're ready to take the risk, don't you?"

That hum inside her grew brighter, hotter. "We're in Las Vegas. What better place for a gamble?"

That amazing smile flashed briefly again. "I'll pick you up at seven."

"Okay." Nodding, she went through the door, closed it behind her and for a couple of fast seconds, leaned back against it to catch her breath. Her legs were still trembling, her heartbeat thundering in her chest and her breath was uneven.

Terri's body was lit up like the neon night in Vegas. She felt the buzz of expectation and knew that she wanted Cooper more now than she had before and that was really saying something.

She'd never been much of a gambler, so maybe here, with Cooper, she'd have a little beginner's luck.

Seven

In all the times Terri had checked into hotels over the years, she'd never really thought about the whole process. She'd never make that mistake again.

Debra Vitale was the assistant manager, a woman in her fifties who'd been with the StarFire hotel for twenty years. She knew everything there was to know about her job and was patient enough to explain it all to Terri.

Debra even walked her through signing in a couple of guests on her own and Terri laughed with the incoming guests, explaining that she was new. And, with the helpful champagne served to those in line, people were, on the most part, patient. When her last guest left the counter, Terri turned to Debra.

"This is a lot more complicated than I ever realized."

"It really is," Debra said, smiling. "But you did a great job."

"I don't know about that, but—"

Two desks down from Terri, Brent, the reservations clerk who had checked *her* into the hotel just a few days ago, was talking to a young couple.

"I'm very sorry," he said apologetically. "We simply don't have a record of your reservation."

Terri's gaze shifted to the couple, each of them holding an untouched glass of champagne. The woman was desperately trying not to cry while her husband—Terri assumed he was her husband—looked frustrated with just a touch of helplessness.

Curious now, Terri started walking over, not surprised when Debra went with her. "Is there a problem?"

"Ms. Ferguson." He said her name like a prayer of gratitude. "There seems to be a mistake here somewhere."

"Who are you?" the man on the other side of the counter asked.

"I'm Terri Ferguson, one of the owners of the StarFire." Wow, she hadn't stumbled on those words at all. "How can I help?"

Almost at the end of his rope, the young man said, "We have a reservation here for a junior suite for two nights." He handed over a printout of his confirmation. While Terri read it, he kept talking. "We're on our honeymoon. Staying here two nights before we fly to Hawaii…" He took a breath and said, "I don't know why you don't have a record of it, but—"

Terri looked from him to the bride at his side and back again. Honeymooners. A twinge of sympathy

grabbed her, then she asked Brent, "Have you checked *everywhere*?"

"Yes, ma'am, I have," he said and Terri still didn't like the sound of *ma'am*. "There's no record of it and—" he lowered his voice "—we don't have any junior suites available. They're all booked."

The lobby and casino were loud, as usual, but all Terri could hear was the quiet sniff of the bride as she fought back tears of disappointment. She knew that Brent and Debra were both watching her, to see how she handled this crisis, so Terri jumped right in.

"Okay," she said, "have we got suites available on the VIP floors?"

Brent's eyes widened, then as he understood where she was going with this, a slow smile curved his mouth until he was grinning at her. "Yes, ma'am, we do."

Terri shot a quick look at Debra and saw the approval in the other woman's eyes. That felt good. It would have convinced her, if she'd had any doubt at all, that she was doing the right thing. What good was owning a couple thousand hotels if you couldn't give away a room now and then?

Brent turned to the computer, hit the keys like a concert pianist and a moment later confirmed, "We've got a two-bedroom suite ready on the twenty-second floor. It's open for the next week."

"Perfect," Terri said and gave his hand a pat. "Print out some keys, will you? Oh, and refund their room deposit, as well. And, we're not charging them for anything."

His eyebrows shot up. "You want their entire stay comped?"

"Is that the word?" She smiled. "Then, yes. Comped. I think when your honeymoon starts off that badly, it takes a little magic to turn things around."

He laughed to himself, shook his head and printed out a set of keys. Then he tucked them into a folder and handed it to her.

"While we're at it," Terri said, "have room service send up a dozen roses and a bottle of champagne. Oh, and good tickets to Darci's show tonight."

"I'll take care of that," Debra said, then murmured, "Well done, *boss*."

Terri grinned.

Brent looked at her, approval clear on his features. "You are a great boss."

"Thank you. Now, let's get this new couple settled." She motioned for the newlyweds to follow her down the length of the counter to the bell stand. There, she signaled one of the bellmen and said, "Please take Mr. and Mrs. Hunter to the twenty-second floor. Suite 2205."

"Yes, ma'am."

Terri sighed. She was clearly going to have to get used to the ma'am thing. Turning to the Hunters, she handed the key packet to the brand-new husband. "We've given you a suite on the VIP floor—"

"We can't afford that," his wife said quickly.

"You don't have to afford it," Terri told her as the noise level around her rose and fell like waves. "Your stay is on the house."

"What?" The new husband looked down at the

folder in his hand, then lifted his gaze to Terri's. "I don't understand."

"It's simple." Terri smiled at both of them, knowing exactly how they felt. It was almost impossible to compute when something completely out of the blue crashed down on you. "The StarFire wants to make it up to you for the reservation problem."

He stared at her, clearly stunned. "I don't know what to say."

"Oh, my God," his bride whispered.

"You don't have to say anything. The StarFire is happy to make this right." At least she was pretty sure Cooper would be good with it. And if he wasn't, well, she *was* a partner, wasn't she? "We wish you a long and happy marriage and a fabulous honeymoon."

"Thank you," the man said and held out one hand. "I can't tell you how much we appreciate this."

"You don't have to try. Be sure to catch the show, too," Terri said. "Darci Ryan is playing in the main theater tonight. The concierge will send your tickets up to the room."

"Tickets to her concert, too?" The bride took a gulp of her champagne.

"This is—" Jack Hunter shook his head, lost for words.

Terri took advantage of his stunned silence. "While you're here, we want you to enjoy yourselves and not worry about a thing." Terri grinned at both of them and loved watching the succession of emotions that crossed their faces.

"I don't know how to thank you," the bride said softly. "You saved the honeymoon."

Terri grinned. "We're happy to help. Be sure to check out our restaurants. They're pretty fabulous. Or room service if you prefer privacy. Just pay as a room charge and you're set. Now, if you'll go with the bellman, he'll show you to your suite."

The bride laughed in delight, threw herself at Terri and gave her a huge hug. "This is amazing. You're amazing. And when we get back home, we're going to tell everyone we've ever met to come to the StarFire. Thank you so much!"

Terri hugged her back, then released her. "You're welcome. Enjoy your stay with us."

"We absolutely will," the groom assured her.

"If you'll follow me…" The bellman took their luggage and started off across the lobby, headed for the private elevator.

Once they were gone, Terri headed back to reservations. She still had plenty to learn, but today was a good start.

Celeste watched the whole performance.

That's how she thought of it. The eager young lovers, saddened and disappointed, and Terri Ferguson riding to the rescue. She hated that she admired what Terri had done.

Something she had noticed over the years: most people in positions of wealth and power lost all sense of the other people around them.

But Terri had seen the problem and solved it in a

lovely way. The honeymooners were cooing at each other and laughing all the way across the lobby and Terri had given that to them. Maybe she was more than Celeste had assumed her to be. And maybe, once she became accustomed to this life, Terri would stop noticing people like the young couple she had just helped.

Celeste wondered, and found herself hoping Terri wouldn't change. Looking at the couple again, she bit back a wave of envy so thick she could hardly draw a breath. She'd wanted that once. A shining kind of love that would last and grow warm as the first flash of heat dissipated. But the world in which she lived didn't *do* love.

Instead, there were quick "relationships" that flamed out as spectacularly as they began. She'd had plenty of those over the years, and Celeste was forced to admit that the closest she'd ever come to more was when she'd been involved with Cooper. Maybe she'd have had a real chance there. But she'd tossed him and the idea of *more* away in favor of an old man with a title and a few more zeroes in his bank accounts. For all the good that had done her.

Her count had died two months before their wedding and his grown children hadn't even waited until after the funeral to show her the door. And since he hadn't changed his will, she'd been left nothing.

Now she was an aging supermodel with a limited number of years to build up her own bank accounts— or to find a man who could give her all of that and more. Was that man Cooper? She couldn't be sure, but until she got rid of Terri, she'd never know.

Terri was younger than Celeste and it was a barb in the throat to realize that she looked it, as well. In her sunshine-yellow dress, Terri looked fresh, innocent almost. While only that morning, Celeste had found a few tiny lines at the corners of her eyes. Lines. Not wrinkles. She would never be wrinkled and lines could be dealt with.

But it was lowering to admit that time was finally catching up with her. Since she'd begun her modeling career fifteen years ago at seventeen, Celeste had been a star. People around the world knew her name and face. Feeling that power slowly coming to an end was something she hated to think about, let alone acknowledge. Men around the world had thrown themselves at her feet and she'd walked across them like rocks in a river, to get where she wanted to be.

Which was one reason she'd come back to Vegas.

Soon, her modeling career would end—either that or she'd be relegated to B-list jobs, which she wouldn't tolerate. So she'd come to Vegas to take Cooper back. She'd planned to come in another month or so, but when Dave called to tell her about the new woman Cooper was interested in, Celeste had advanced her arrival.

Now it was time to make Cooper see that Terri would never truly belong in his world. Forcing a smile, she walked across the lobby, loving the slide of her black silk pants across her skin.

At the long, marble-topped counter, she caught Terri's eye and motioned for her to come over.

"Celeste, hi. What're you doing here?"

Around them, people noticed her, whispering, and Celeste instinctively posed for them, tossing her hair back from her face.

"I've come to take you shopping," she said. "The hotel limo is waiting for us outside."

"Oh. I can't go now. I'm really busy here and—"

"Terri," Celeste sighed a little. Was the woman really this earnest? "You are the owner. You may come and go as you please. And as the owner, you need to go shopping. You have a responsibility to look the part you're living."

Terri looked down at her simple yellow dress and then to Celeste. "I could use some new things, I suppose. I'm going to dinner with Cooper tonight and—"

Celeste used every ounce of her legendary self-control to hide the irritation she felt at Terri's statement. A dinner date with Cooper. To be followed, no doubt, by simple Utah sex.

All the better, she told herself. This was the plan. Celeste Vega was an experienced, wildly inventive lover. Once Cooper had slept with Terri, and indulged in vanilla sex, the pretty blonde would never hold up in comparison to Celeste.

"Excellent. Let's go, then." Celeste started walking, fully expecting Terri to follow her. The quick click of heels against the glimmering floor tiles behind her, told Celeste she was right. "I thought we'd start at the Grand Canal Shoppes at the Venetian."

"We have shops here in the StarFire, too."

"Yes, but we can't ride in the limo to these shops. Or drink the champagne waiting for us."

Terri laughed a little at that, then said, "But I need my purse. My credit cards..."

"You must start thinking like the owner of the StarFire," Celeste ordered, threading her arm through Terri's just to keep her walking. "You'll charge everything to the hotel and have it delivered to your suite."

"Oh, but—"

"In this," Celeste commanded, *"trust me."*

Two hours later Celeste had to admit that she'd enjoyed herself more than she had expected to. Usually, the people Celeste was with had their own agendas. Terri didn't. She didn't want anything from her. Wasn't trying to use her to advance her career. She was...nice. Sweet, even.

And that in itself was enough to make Celeste feel off balance.

"Is it always like this for you?" Terri asked.

"What do you mean?" Leaving the Grand Canal Shoppes, where cobblestone paths wended past tidy shops where flowers spilled in bright splashes of color, they walked across one of the stone bridges that spanned a canal where gondolas sailed. October sunshine was warm, but not hot, and a soft wind blew in from the desert.

"People have been taking pictures of you for the past couple of hours."

"Oh." Strange, she'd hardly noticed. Was it that Celeste was just so used to the attention? Or had she been having such a good time, it hadn't registered? "Yes, it's one of the downsides of celebrity. You can't even

leave your house without makeup on or you're on the front page of a tabloid looking like the wrath of God."

"It's gotta be weird to live like that, isn't it? You can't even go shopping without being watched." Terri smiled tightly at a woman aiming her phone at them. "It's like you're never really alone."

"You get used to it."

"I don't think I could."

"I didn't either, once," Celeste admitted, remembering a younger version of herself who had railed against every tiny dig into her privacy. "And now I don't remember what it was like to be invisible."

Terri shifted one of her shopping bags to her right hand. Celeste noticed. "You could have had those bags delivered to the hotel along with the rest."

Smiling, Terri said, "I know, but I just wanted to carry the red dress and shoes with me. I've never owned anything so gorgeous and you know, I wouldn't have bought that dress if you weren't there. Incredible how expensive it was considering there's so little fabric to it."

Celeste laughed. "It looked wonderful on you." Too good, actually, but if she was to get Cooper's attention back on *her*, then she needed him to get Terri into his bed so he could be bored.

Hmm. Perhaps Dave was right after all. Her plan did sound wildly convoluted. But she was committed now.

"Do you like it?" Terri asked. "The attention?"

Celeste looked at her and saw genuine interest in Terri's eyes. She couldn't remember the last time she and one of her "friends" had had a real conversation.

Usually, it was about this man or that party. But Terri had been talking to her for two solid hours, asking questions and actually listening to the answers.

And Celeste wasn't sure what to do with that. Terri wasn't really her friend. Celeste didn't *have* friends anymore. She had air-kissed strangers flitting in and out of her life and she'd become so accustomed to that superficial life, Celeste hardly knew how to respond to reality.

"If I didn't like being noticed," she finally said, "I went into the wrong business."

"I suppose." Terri lifted the bags she held and changed the subject. "Anyway, I appreciate you taking me shopping."

"It was fun," Celeste said, again surprising herself with the admission. In fact, she couldn't remember the last time she'd enjoyed herself so much. Terri talked to everyone. Salespeople, tourists, other shoppers. The barista who'd prepared their cappuccinos had been half in love with her by the time they left.

Celeste had signed autographs for a couple of people and then laughed with Terri over some truly hideous fashion offerings in the shops. She'd told her about growing up in San Diego, California, and how she'd been "discovered" by a modeling agent while she was playing volleyball at the beach. Terri had told her all about growing up in Utah and had made it sound lovely enough that Celeste was tempted to go and see it for herself.

All in all, it had been a very different kind of afternoon for Celeste. Spending time with another woman

without the inherent jealousy and backbiting of her profession had been...fun. And there was that word again.

Yes. She was definitely unsettled.

The StarFire limo was waiting for them and within fifteen minutes, the two women had been whisked back to the hotel. In the lobby, Terri gave her a tight hug. "Thanks so much, Celeste. It was good to get out of the hotel and feel a little normal—even if this is a brand-new kind of normal. I'm still sort of having a heart attack over the prices of these things."

"Terri," Celeste said with a sigh, "you're half owner of a company worth billions. It's time you started dressing the part."

Nodding, Terri said, "I know you're right, but I still feel a little guilty. Without you along, I would have headed to the mall, not the Grand Canal."

With high drama, Celeste clutched her heart. "Now you're going to give *me* an attack. The *mall*? Never." Giving her a smile, Celeste said briskly, "Oh, and thanks to *you*, I have several new things that I'm going to look spectacular in."

Terri laughed. "I know you will. Now, I think I'll go upstairs. I'll see you later?"

"Of course." Celeste watched the other woman hurry across the crowded lobby toward the private elevator. And she was surprised to realize that a part of her was sad to see Terri go.

Up in Cooper's office, Dave Carey was frustrated and furious.

"Thousands," Dave said, holding out the stack of re-

ceipts. "The two of them spent *thousands* at the Grand
Canal Shoppes and charged it all to the hotel."

Cooper took the receipts and idly flipped through
them. "I'm guessing Celeste is behind the more expensive items," he murmured.

"Does it matter whose is whose?" Dave threw both
hands high. Accounting had sent him the stack of receipts from some of Las Vegas's finest shops and he'd
been riding on fury ever since. Yeah, Celeste had told
him her plans, but she hadn't said they were going to
go through nearly fifty thousand dollars. *Most* of it
spent on Celeste herself.

Her "plan" clearly wasn't working. Terri Ferguson
was supposed to be feeling out of place here. Instead, it
seemed to Dave as though she was settling in. Getting
pretty damn cozy with the idea of being a billionaire.
In fact, it was starting to look like they were all going
to be stuck with Terri.

"Your new 'partner' doesn't seem to have any trouble living it up on the company's dime. She didn't *earn*
this, but she's got no problem spending like she did."
Dave looked at Cooper and waited for the flash of fury
he was sure would be coming.

But Cooper only shrugged and tossed the stack of
papers onto his desk. "She didn't buy a damn jet, Dave.
It's some clothes."

"Celeste went shopping, too—"

"Celeste *always* shops." Shaking his head, Cooper
said, "A few thousand to keep her out of my hair seems
like a good deal to me."

"Seriously?" Dave whirled around, walked a few

paces away, then stomped right back to the edge of Cooper's desk. "You're actually okay with this? What happened to *get the new partner out of town as fast as possible*? Buy her out? What happened to *that* plan?"

Cooper gave him a cool stare, but Dave wasn't fooled. He saw the fire behind the ice in Cooper's eyes, and Dave took a mental step back. If he pushed his old friend too hard at the wrong moment, he could ruin the whole thing for himself. He had to handle this carefully, keep reminding Cooper that the two of them were on the same side.

"I don't answer to you, Dave," Cooper said softly.

"I know that." Dave held up both hands in a peace-making gesture. He eased back in his tone and body language. "I'm just thinking about the future, Cooper. This is your company she's trying to horn in on."

"She's half owner whether either one of us likes it or not."

Dave didn't. "She's trying to change too much too soon."

Cooper leaned back in his desk chair and stared up at him. "How long should she wait?"

"You know what I mean," Dave countered and felt himself losing this particular battle. "Hell, I thought we were on the same page on this."

"We are."

"Then why are you okay with family-style hotels and thousands spent at boutiques?"

"You ever hear of a long game, Dave?" Cooper stood up. Eye to eye with his old friend, he continued, "I'm giving her time to see that this isn't what she wants.

Shopping doesn't bother me. The family hotel thing might be a good idea. But one good idea doesn't mean she's going to make this her career. Her life. Once she realizes that, she'll take the offer of a buyout more easily."

"Seems to me she's having too good a time to give it all up now." Dave pushed one hand through his hair and fought a fresh wave of frustration. Had Cooper so completely let his own desires take hold that he didn't notice when the woman was entrenching herself?

"A few thousand dollars on clothes isn't going to make a difference here, Dave. She'll leave. Eventually."

Eventually.

Dave gritted his teeth to keep from saying more. Friends or not, Cooper was the boss and there was only so much he would be willing to put up with.

"Take the receipts back to accounting." Cooper walked across the office to the window affording an incredible view of the Vegas Strip. "Make sure they know to approve any purchases made by Terri."

"Right." Dave swept up the papers and curled them in one tight fist. At the door, he paused and turned when Cooper called his name. "Yeah?"

His gaze was hard, cool. "Leave Terri to me, Dave. Is that clear?"

"Couldn't be clearer," he said and walked out. With the door closed behind him, Dave swallowed back a rising fury. His plans were crumbling because Cooper had a hard-on for the woman currently screwing them all over.

Damned if he'd leave it to the man who couldn't see past his own dick.

Eight

Several hours later Cooper couldn't find it in him to be mad about the thousands of dollars Terri had spent at the Venetian. At least, not when she was wearing the smallest, tightest, sexiest red dress he'd ever seen. It was strapless, exposing the tops of her breasts to his hungry eyes. It was tight, skimming her figure like a lover's hands. And it was so damn short, it was just barely legal. Her long, tanned legs looked silky smooth, and the red heels she wore seemed designed to keep a man's gaze fixed on those legs.

They'd been to dinner at the hotel's best restaurant, attended Darci Ryan's concert and now they were having a drink in the hotel's top bar. All very civilized. Except he felt more like a man on the edge of a precipice. Slipping over that edge could make for a long,

dangerous fall. If he got involved with Terri wouldn't that throw a wrench into his plans? Did he care?

He had a sip of his scotch and said, "So I hear you gave away a two-night stay in a VIP suite?"

She went perfectly still and actually looked guilty. "Is that a problem?"

Cooper stared at her as she took a sip of her wine. "Problem? I don't know. You realize those suites go for five thousand a night."

Terri choked on her wine and fought for breath, slapping at her own chest. "*Dollars? Five thousand dollars?* Really? How do we justify charging so much money for basically a place to sleep?"

Wryly, Cooper said, "It's a little more than a cot with a single wool blanket."

"Well, sure, but seriously?"

"Views that can't be beat, top-notch security and twenty-four-hour butler service? Media rooms? VIP seats at concerts, in-house massages…"

She took another sip of her wine and Cooper watched her throat work as she swallowed. It shouldn't have been sexy, but it was. Hell, he was discovering that everything about Terri Ferguson was sexy. Even just *thinking* about her could make him as hard and eager as a damn horny teenager. Being this close to her was a kind of torture.

"Wow." She whispered the word and shook her head as if she still couldn't believe the cost of the room she'd comped. "Okay, well the room was going to be empty all week, anyway. So let's just say that we're letting

the Hunters stay there to check it out. Make sure the suite is in good shape."

"Yeah," he said, mouth twitching as he listened to her try to justify the comp. "We already know that."

She grinned. "Now we'll be sure."

When he didn't say anything, simply continued to watch her, Terri sighed. "Okay. They were on their honeymoon. Their reservation got lost. The bride was crying and nobody should cry on their honeymoon and—"

"It was a nice thing to do," he said. He'd have probably done the same thing himself ten years ago. These days, though, he was too involved upstairs to spend much time in the heart of the hotel.

She beamed at him. "Really?"

"Great PR, too. They'll tell everyone they know about the StarFire and the owner who saved their honeymoon."

"We sent them champagne and roses, too," she told him.

He actually laughed. "Naturally."

She tossed her long blond hair behind her shoulders, and he watched the bosom of that dress like a hawk, half expecting her breasts to pop out the next time she took a deep breath. Even as he thought it, though, he smiled to himself. Never gonna happen, but a man could dream.

"I like the dress."

"What? Oh." She laughed a little uneasily and ran her fingers across the bodice as if checking to make

sure it was in place. "Thanks. It's gorgeous, isn't it? Celeste picked it out."

"Of course she did," he mused. Celeste settled for nothing less than the best—especially when someone else was paying for it. "Did you like the show?"

Her eyes lit up. "It was wonderful. And going backstage to meet Darci? Amazing. She's so nice, too. I didn't expect that, but maybe I should have." She shrugged. "Just because someone's famous doesn't mean they're unfriendly. Celeste has been really nice to me even though you and she used to—"

Her voice trailed off so he finished the sentence for her. "Be lovers." He watched her teeth tug at her lower lip while she thought of something to say.

Finally, she asked, "How long ago?"

"She left almost two years ago. Why?"

"*She* left you?"

"Yeah. Again. Why?"

"Just…" She paused, took a breath that brought those breasts closer to spilling out of the red, silky fabric. "I guess I wanted to know if you were done with her before—"

"Before I take you upstairs to bed?"

"Before we take each other." Her gaze met his and he had to admit, he still liked her style of being blunt. Cutting right to the point.

"It's not her I'm thinking about," he said.

"That's good." She shifted in her chair, sliding those long legs against each other until he had to make a fist to keep from reaching out and stroking her skin.

They were in the StarBar on the nineteenth floor.

The views out the three hundred sixty-degree windows were incredible, and the crowd mobbing the place showed Cooper just how popular this spot was. No loud music making conversations impossible. There was a gleaming black piano in one corner and one talented pianist keeping waves of notes rolling through the crowd. And suddenly, he was wishing he'd taken her to the roof instead. Where they could have a private drink. Where he could touch her as he wanted to.

They had a booth at the back of the room and still there was a wide view of the night sky and the echoes of neon from far below.

"So what *are* you thinking right now?" she asked.

"All kinds of interesting things." His gaze locked with hers and he saw the flash of response in her eyes.

Another deep breath and all Cooper could think was he was another quarter inch of fabric away from having her breasts tumble free.

And into those delicious thoughts came Dave's voice, his warning, the reminder of what this was all about. But, Cooper assured himself, as he silenced his friend's cautionary words, he had lost sight of nothing.

Terri was here, so he'd deal with her until she wasn't.

Sooner or later she would go. Once she realized she was out of her depth and wouldn't be able to tread water indefinitely. Which was perfect for him. He liked his relationships as temporary as a jackpot win. But for now, everything else had to take a backseat to what was happening between them.

For days the tension between them had been tighten-

ing. Every touch, every glance, was filled with enough sexual heat to start a bonfire.

And tonight they'd feel the flames.

She finished off her glass of white wine, licked her top lip in a deliberately slow, sensuous manner, then said, "Show me."

He stood up, took her hand and pulled her from her chair. Even as tall as she was, despite the amazing heels she wore, he looked down into her eyes and Cooper felt a jolt of heat so vicious, it stole his breath. "Let's go."

He kept a tight grip on her hand and Terri's fingers were curled just as tightly around his. She kept up with his hurried strides across the bar and that told him she was as eager as he to finally sate the hunger.

They were almost to the private elevator when Cooper heard it.

"Mr. Hayes!"

"Dammit." He gritted his teeth and drew Terri to a stop before turning to face a security guard walking toward him. He read the man's name badge and asked, "What is it, Guthrie?"

"Sorry to interrupt, sir." In his forties, he was ex-military and kept his blond hair in the buzz cut he must prefer. "We've got a couple cheats, boss."

"Someone's *cheating*?" Terri looked from one to the other of them and Cooper almost laughed at her shocked expression.

"Yeah, we get them." He frowned at the admission. "It's not easy cheating the system in Vegas, and we've got plenty of security and surveillance that cuts

it down, but there's always *someone* who thinks he's got it figured out."

Guthrie nodded at Terri before turning back to Cooper. "The twenty-one dealer alerted the pit boss about the card counter. Guy wasn't even trying to hide it. Can't figure if he's ballsy or just stupid. Anyway, we've got him locked down. Security will grab him when he tries to leave the floor."

In a weird way, Cooper almost admired card counters. At least they were willing to work for it. Though it wasn't strictly cheating, most casinos didn't allow card counters because it was too easy for them to judge the odds on betting.

"Okay, and…" Cooper tightened his grip on Terri's hand. He really didn't need all of this right now.

"The other cheat? Looks like he's using a new technique on a video poker machine. Guy's hit four jackpots in the last two hours."

Cooper frowned. "Same machine?"

"Same jackpots, too." Guthrie nodded. "The guy's hit four deuces with a three kicker twice."

"That's impossible," Terri whispered. "The odds are—"

"How do you know that?" Cooper watched her.

"I like math. And that's way out of the realm of possible."

"We think so, too, ma'am," Guthrie said. "We've got the guy pinned under the eye in the sky, but if he bolts, he's leaving with a lot of cash and the secret to his success."

Irritated as hell, Cooper turned to Terri. "I've got to handle this."

"Should I come?"

Tempting, but— "No. You go on up. I'll let you know what happens as soon as I can."

"Okay." Terri gave his hand a hard squeeze before taking the private elevator to the owner's floor.

Cooper and Guthrie took another elevator to the third floor, where the surveillance room and a wall full of computer monitors waited for them. This was *not* how he'd planned on spending his night.

"I want this handled fast," Cooper muttered as they walked into the heartbeat of the StarFire. Damned if he'd let Fate interrupt he and Terri again.

"Don't blame you, boss," Guthrie murmured and quickly led the way to where they were watching the cheat.

An hour later a card counter had been escorted out of the casino and a brilliant cheat with an electro-magnet had been arrested. Cooper was done dealing with people. He'd had enough of the noise and the crowds. All he wanted now was to get back to Terri. To finish what they'd been promising each other for days.

He'd brought a bottle of champagne and a pocketful of condoms with him, but Terri didn't answer her door. He knocked again with the same result and wondered if she'd gone to bed. Then he remembered the look in her eyes and told himself no way. Shaking his head, he walked back to his own apartment, then out onto the balcony. A cold, sharp wind blew at him, easing

over the edge of the Plexiglas to ruffle his hair. But it didn't do a damn thing to the fires burning inside him.

Her balcony doors were open, so Cooper walked into the living room of her suite. Lamplight created puddles of gold in the darkness as if she'd left them burning for him in welcome. He went down the hall to her bedroom, found another lamp burning there. Light and the muffled purr of tub jets drifted through the open bathroom door and Cooper headed for it.

He shrugged out of his suit jacket and tossed it onto the nearest chair. Setting the champagne bottle down on the dresser, he tore his tie off and opened his collar button. He could breathe easier now, but his heart was pounding and his body felt hard and heavy.

Scent reached him first. It was light, airy, like a summer morning. Then he saw the billowing steam lifting off the bathtub and finally, he saw *her*. She had her hair bundled up high on her head and she was stretched out in the tub while powerful jets hummed and frothed the bubble bath she'd added to the water into a mountain of soap bubbles. She looked like a damn fairy. Unreal. Mystical.

And he wanted her so badly, he was choking on the need.

Her eyes were closed, until he said simply, "Terri."

She didn't jolt in surprise. Instead, she slowly turned her head and opened her eyes to look at him. "I wondered when you'd get here."

"Sorry I'm late," he said, smiling in spite of the tension gripping him.

She pushed up a little higher in the tub, finally giv-

ing him a good look at those breasts of hers, dotted now with bubbles.

"I figured you'd find the open doors..."

"Good guess."

"So why are you still dressed?"

"Good question," he muttered and tore his shirt off. While she watched, he undressed quickly, then stepped into the tub and hissed. "You *like* boiling?"

She grinned up at him. "I like it hot."

"Now that, I take as a direct challenge."

"Excellent." She smiled and the fairy-like image intensified. Covered in bubbles, strands of blond hair falling out of the topknot on her head and those big blue eyes watching him, she was, at the moment, *everything*.

Lowering into the water, Cooper felt the jets blast against his back as he levered himself over her, taking her mouth with a hunger that surprised even him. She reached up and encircled his neck, pulling him down to her, parting her legs and wrapping them around his hips.

The wet glide of his skin against hers set his nerve endings on fire. He'd waited. Wanted. And now he would have.

Cooper filled his hands with her breasts, stroking his thumbs across her hardened nipples until she was writhing beneath him and the hot water churned and splashed up both sides of the tub. She tipped her head back against the edge and stared blankly up at the ceiling. Running her hands up and down his back, fingernails dragging along his spine, she groaned his name. Cooper dipped his head, took one of those perfect pink

nipples into his mouth and rolled his tongue across the tip. She gasped and arched high, her legs still locked around his hips.

Cooper fought the urge to slide into her heat right then. But damned if he'd complicate things further with an unintended pregnancy. They'd have to wait for a bed to complete this, but for now he could torment them both even further.

He lifted his head and shifted quickly, spinning her around until he was behind her—her back to his front. Her butt was a temptation he ignored. For now. Hot water pulsed against his back as the jets, on high, pummeled the water and their bodies.

Cooper kissed her neck, ran his hands across her breasts and down her sides, sliding across her abdomen, to her center, then to those long, lovely legs.

"Cooper…" Her head against his chest, she turned her face up to his. Her eyes were glassy, her lips parted into a hungry pout that tore at him. "Cooper, what're you—"

"You'll see…" He held her thighs open and slid closer to one of the tub's jets. As soon as that rushing hot water hit her center, Terri jolted in his arms.

"Cooper!" His name came out as a helpless shriek. The water pulsed, her body moved and she breathed, heavy, fast, rocking her hips into the source of her torment. And he watched it all. Watched her strain and reach for the orgasm that was inching closer and closer. He'd never seen anything as totally sexual as Terri moving in the bubble-filled water, finding pleasure in the swirling heat.

Lifting her arms, she reached back and brought his head down to hers. While the water pounded against her core, she dragged his mouth to hers and kissed him breathlessly, desperately. He held her, their mouths fused, their breaths mingling and when the hot, frothy water finally pushed her over the edge, he tasted her surrender and had never known anything sweeter.

When her body finally stopped trembling, Cooper spun her around in his arms again, lifting her legs to hook them around his hips. With one quick move, he could be inside her, buried so deep within that it might possibly ease the incredible ache that had been tearing at him for days. And because he was no more than a breath away from doing just that, Cooper muttered, "That's it."

"What? What's it?" She threw her head back and looked at him through passion-glazed eyes.

He stood up, still holding her to him, her legs around his waist. "We stay here another second, I'm going to take you in this tub."

"And that's bad?" she asked dreamily.

"Without a condom it is," he snapped, really close to saying *screw it* and getting on with things.

That registered fast. "Right. You have one? A condom? Or two?"

"I do." He stepped out of the tub and a wave of water sloshed out behind them.

"We're making a hideous mess," she complained, glancing down at the water pooling on the green tile.

"Housekeeping," he muttered, and snatched up his slacks on the way to the bedroom.

"Right. Good point."

The French doors were still open to the night and a soft wind slipped inside, brushing across their wet skin, making them both shiver. But Cooper was past caring. There was only so much torture a man could take. Only so much waiting. He walked to the wide bed, dropped Terri onto the mattress where she bounced with a laugh that rippled through the lamp-lit shadows and made him smile in spite of everything. He grabbed a condom from his pocket, tore it open and sheathed himself faster than he ever had before.

And then finally he was where he'd wanted to be almost from the first moment he saw her. Cooper covered her body with his and when she lifted her legs to pull him in, he followed. He pushed himself deep inside her and as she gasped, he sighed at the sense of completion that swamped him. Tightly inside her heat, he held perfectly still for a long moment or two, just to savor the sensation.

Then his body took over and he moved within her, creating a rhythm that she eagerly matched. Their bodies sliding together in perfect harmony, their harsh breaths echoing in the stillness. Desperation fueled desire, and desire flashed into an almost unbearable heat.

He watched her face, saw everything she was feeling written there and knew that he would never tire of seeing her like this. Of knowing what they could build together. Days of wanting, thinking, needing, combined to bring them both rushing toward climax. It was going too fast and he knew it. Sensed it. He wanted to make it all last longer, to drag this out forever, but

he couldn't wait another second. And the sounds of her moans and gasps told him she felt the same. There would be time again for slow and torturous. Tonight they needed satisfaction.

Faster, higher, they chased each other up the mountain until the peak was within reach and then, locked together, they flew over the top and held on to each other all the way down.

A couple of minutes later Cooper's head cleared of the lust-driven fog he'd been living under for days. He was staggered. Shaken. Nothing he'd ever known had prepared him for what had just happened and damn, if that didn't put the fear of God into a man. His control of any given situation was what he prided himself on. But with Terri, his instinct was to throw control out the closest window.

What the hell was he supposed to do with that?

But in the next second he reassured himself that what he was feeling was only because Terri was new to his life. She was at once an innocent and wildly receptive. She was different from every other woman he knew. She was open, kind, funny and didn't really care about the money or power she now commanded.

What he had to do was get used to having her, being with her. Then these...*feelings* would fade and he could send her back to Utah with a smile on his face. He congratulated himself silently on once again taking the reins in the situation. He felt a little better about everything.

When he was fairly certain he could move without

collapsing, he rolled to one side and draped one hand across his belly.

Next to him, Terri went up on her elbow and looked down at him. "That was amazing."

"You really like that word, don't you?" He gave her a quick smile, because what else could he do? Her hair was a tumble of waves and curls, her lips were swollen from so many hungry kisses and the curve of her mouth hit him hard.

"Sometimes, it's the only one that fits." She licked her lips and sent a jolt of fire to his belly and Cooper knew he was still in dangerous territory.

"This one time, I'll agree with you." But he wouldn't stay lying there beside her. If he did, he'd take her again and that wasn't going to help him get his head on straight. He pushed off the bed and stalked to the bathroom. Cleaned up, he tossed a few towels onto the floor to soak up the flood, then reached down to turn off the tub jets.

On his way back into the bedroom, he snatched his slacks and pulled them on.

Terri sat up in the bed and looked even more fairy-like now. The bed was huge and she looked so small in it. A single lamp tossed just enough light to make the shadows deeper and to somehow highlight her. Her blond hair tumbled down over her shoulders and onto her breasts, and his hands itched to cup them again.

Danger, his mind shouted. *Get out while you can.*

"You're leaving already?"

"Yeah." He was leaving now, while he could still convince himself to go. But he had to say something.

To head off at the pass any thoughts that this might be more than what it was—satisfying sex. "Look, Terri, I don't want you to—"

She tipped her head to one side, her long hair sliding off her shoulders to swing free like a golden curtain. Holding up one hand for quiet, she finished his sentence for him. "Get stars in my eyes? Hire a wedding planner and pick out a sweet little bungalow built for two?"

He stopped pulling his clothes on, leaving his dress shirt hanging open. Staring at her, he tried to figure out what she was thinking. Feeling. Was he somehow completely wrong about what was rushing through her mind? Usually about now, whatever woman he was with started sighing romantically and hinting that if they were so good together they should *stay* together. Be a couple. Be engaged. Then married. But he'd already discovered Terri was like no one he'd ever known.

Hell, for all he knew, she hadn't enjoyed any of this. No. Bull. He knew when a woman had a damn orgasm, and hers had rocked both of them. So what was she up to?

"Yeah," he said. "I didn't say that."

"You didn't have to." She scooted off the bed and naked, she walked right up to him. His mouth watered. He wanted her again. Now. "God, Cooper, do you really think you're completely unreadable? Panic was shining in your eyes so brightly I could have read a book by it."

No one had ever seen through him so easily before. "I don't panic."

"Not about much, probably, but this, yes." She slid her hands up his chest, her fingers defining every ridge of every muscle. Heat spiraled from her touch, soaking through his skin to burn up his bones. Then her thumbs moved over his flat nipples and he hissed in a breath as he fought for control.

"But you don't have to worry," she continued, sliding his shirt down off his arms to let it fall to the floor. "I didn't fall madly in love in an instant."

"I didn't say you did."

"And, if I promise not to propose, will you stay?"

Well, didn't he feel like an idiot? Cooper was used to being the one to hand out the after-sex cautionary tale. Felt weird to be on the receiving end and he didn't much like it. But damned if he didn't admire her for it. "Blunt. No BS. I still like that about you."

"Here's more blunt," she said, going up on her toes to slant her mouth over his in an all too brief kiss. "How many condoms did you bring?"

Nine

A slow smile curved his mouth as he dipped into one of his pockets and came up with a handful of gold foil packets.

"I do like a man who comes prepared." Terri felt the rush of pure, feminine power as she saw the flash of heat in his eyes. Taking one of the packets, she opened it, then unzipped his slacks, found him hard and ready and slowly slid the thin layer of latex along his length.

She watched his silent battle for control and loved that she had been able to bring this strong man to a place of vulnerability. While her fingers curled around him, he pushed his slacks down and kicked them aside. Smiling to herself, she knew he wasn't going anywhere. Not yet, anyway.

"I've got to have you again," he muttered.

"Just what I wanted to hear," she whispered.

He scooped her up into his arms and stalked across the bedroom. She could really get used to being carried by Cooper Hayes. At the bed he sat down and settled her on his lap. Instantly, Terri sighed at the feel of him rubbing against a tender spot, still trembling with her last climax. She was greedy and she was okay with that. She wanted more and wasn't afraid to show him how much.

Moving on him, she swiveled her hips, teasing, almost taking him inside, then pulling back, torturing them both with the hunger that gnawed at their souls. His ice-blue eyes were swimming with heat and she knew hers looked the same. There was something vibrant and powerful between them. She'd never known that sex could be this good. Always before, it had been a soft, almost sweet experience, with a muffled ripple of pleasure to cap it off.

But with Cooper, there was magic. There was an explosion of sensation that left her trembling even as she ached to feel it all again.

His hands closed on her hips; his gaze pinned hers. "No more playing, Terri." He tipped her over onto her back and loomed over her.

But before he could, Terri rolled over onto her belly and lifted her hips off the mattress. Looking back at him over her shoulder, she whispered brokenly, "Be inside me, Cooper."

"You're killing me," he admitted.

She grinned and wiggled her hips. "That is so not the plan."

Cooper moved to kneel behind her and closed his hands over her butt. She groaned as his strong fingers kneaded her flesh, then he slipped one hand down to stroke that hot, desperate core of hers. Her hips moved of their own accord, rocking, swaying, as her body looked for what only he could give her.

Curling her fingers into the meadow-green duvet, Terri lifted her hips higher and held her breath until he pushed himself deeply into her body. He moved with long, sure strokes, pushing her along the path to completion at a breathless pace. She moved into him, taking him so deep, she thought he almost became a part of her. Again and again, he took her, pushing her, claiming her. His hands held her steady and still the world rocked around her.

She tipped her head back and moaned, hearing the hunger in her own voice. Her body coiled tightly. Anticipation heightened every thrust he made because she was that much closer to the explosion she was reaching for. This was more than just physical, her mind whispered. He wasn't simply taking over her body, but he was sliding into her heart, as well. She felt something deep, something overwhelming for him. But she just couldn't think about that now. At this moment, all she wanted in her mind was what he was doing to her body. What he was making her feel. But one day soon, she was going to have to deal with this new development.

He breathed fast and hard, and Terri heard his desperation as clearly as she felt her own. When the first ripple began deep inside her, she quivered in response, pushed back against him and shouted his name. In re-

action, Cooper pushed himself even deeper into her heat and Terri's vision went dark under the strength of the orgasm that hit her. She called his name again and rode the waves that crashed inside her.

Her body was still trembling when she felt him stiffen, heard him shout and then his body, too, was shattering and the world tipped crazily one more time.

Terri could hardly look at Cooper over the conference table the next afternoon. If she did, she was sure everyone at the meeting would see what she was thinking. And she couldn't *stop* thinking about the night before.

It had been magical. Incredible. They'd gone through every one of the condoms he'd brought to her room and they'd finally given in to exhaustion as dawn touched the sky. When she woke up, Terri was alone with her memories and rumpled sheets. She hadn't heard from Cooper all day and now they were here, in the conference room, sitting at opposite ends of the table from each other as if they were strangers.

Her stomach spun; her mind kept replaying the things he had done to her and with her all night and yet, in his eyes, she saw a cool indifference that she didn't understand.

"So," Cooper demanded, his voice shattering her thoughts and bringing her back to the moment at hand. She was about to find out if her family vacation idea would be approved or not. "Ethan. What'd you find out?"

The man shot Terri an apologetic look before say-

ing, "Surprisingly enough, I found that the numbers bear out the family vacation angle. I wouldn't have thought so many people were dragging their children to Europe, but they are. And it's not just families." He paused, checked his notes, then continued. "As Terri suggested, there are more and more seniors doing extensive traveling. Most of them seem to prefer organized tour groups where reservations and luggage and itinerary are taken care of for them.

"If we work in tandem with those tour organizations, it would be a profitable angle for a Hayes 2. Heck, we could even offer our own tours—maybe offer a stay at two or more of our hotels. They'd come flocking to us for, as Terri put it, 'affordable luxury.'"

Terri let out a breath she hadn't realized she'd been holding. Then Cooper asked, "Sharon?"

"Ethan's right. He brought the numbers to me and together, we dug deeper. There is a demand for the kind of thing Terri suggested. Actually," she added apologetically, "I can't believe none of us considered this before. You asked me to look for locations and I've found several possibilities in Chelsea, Kensington or Knightsbridge for the first Hayes 2." She turned to look at Terri with a new respect in her gaze. "How do you feel about it, Terri?"

Delighted with how this had gone, Terri spoke with more confidence than she'd had the day before. She'd also done some research on family-friendly areas, so she said, "Any of those options sound great, but I'd prefer Kensington. Why don't you see what properties are available and we can go forward from there?"

"I'll get right on it," Sharon said. "And if it's okay with you, I'll bring what I find to your office tomorrow."

Again, Terri felt a rush of pleasure and now it was mixed with pride and a terrific sense of accomplishment. Whatever else happened, she'd at least earned the respect of the people at this table.

"That would be great, thanks. Around two?"

"Perfect," Sharon said.

"All right," Cooper spoke up then. "Is there anything else to cover?"

Everyone began to gather their things, but Terri's voice stopped them in their tracks.

"Actually," she said and every head in the room turned to look at her. Cooper raised one eyebrow as he waited for what she had to say.

"With all of the research I've been doing on European hotels, I noticed that they all offer tea and coffee services in their rooms. This includes a small hot pot along with instant coffee, a variety of tea bags and packages of a few cookies."

"Yes…" Cooper drew that one word out until it was almost three.

"I know we do that here, too, in the more expensive rooms. Why not carry it through to all the rooms?" Terri looked from one face to the other, waiting for a reaction. She didn't have to wait long.

"Because," Eli pointed out, "our guests now order room service coffee. Or go down to the coffee station in the casino where they'll spend even more money."

"True," Terri argued, because she'd already consid-

ered that. "But if they had enough in their rooms to make one cup of coffee, they'd still need room service. I checked with hospitality and the coffee most usually ordered is a full pot, which is six cups. No one who wants that much coffee will be dissuaded by the offer of one free one. And, they'll have coffee to get them through the wait for more."

Eli's mouth worked as if he wanted to disagree, but couldn't find a way to do it.

"And," Terri pointed out, "a couple of cookies won't be breakfast, so they'll still go downstairs to the coffee station. Still stop to throw money into a slot machine. They'll just be in a better mood when they get there."

Someone snorted a laugh.

"It's a good idea," Cooper said.

"Thanks." Terri looked directly at him. His gaze locked with hers even as he spoke in general to the room at large.

"Ethan, put someone on this. I know we've got a lot of the supplies on site now, so I'd like hospitality to work with housekeeping to take care of this."

"Today?" Ethan asked, surprised at the sudden decision.

"Why not today?" Terri asked.

"Exactly," Cooper declared. "Why hesitate on a good idea? I want coffee and tea setups in every room by the end of the week." Cooper stood up and looked at Ethan. "We'll need more hot pots, so contact the restaurant supply companies. Go outside Vegas for supplies if you have to. Work with housekeeping to get this taken care of ASAP."

"Yes, sir." Ethan shot Terri a look of respect, then stood up. "I'm on it."

Everyone else stood, too, and one by one, they left the room, until it was just Cooper and Terri alone again. His gaze was locked on hers, but he didn't speak. Didn't give away any indication of where his thoughts were.

Didn't he feel anything after last night? Had he deliberately shut it all down? Why?

Diffused sunlight poured through the tinted windows lining the conference room. Silence stretched between them until she simply couldn't take it anymore. "You should have woken me when you left."

He shook his head, but he never broke eye contact. "No point in you being awake, too."

Sounded reasonable, but Terri thought there was more to it. "Are you sure that's the reason?"

"What else would it be?" He stood up, shoved his hands in his pockets and kept the ice in his eyes as he looked at her.

What the heck had happened? Where was the heat? Where was the man who'd shown her exactly what her body was capable of? She'd gone her whole life thinking sex was a nice pastime. Now she knew it was so much more when you were with the right man. Was he regretting what they'd shared? And again, *why*?

Terri walked toward him and he didn't back up. He didn't have to. The distance in his eyes was powerful enough.

"I think you were just trying to avoid me."

He snorted and shook his head. "No."

"Cooper—" She reached out to touch his arm, and this time, he did pull back.

"Terri," he ground out, "this isn't the time. We've both got things to do. Last night's over. This is today."

"Wow. And you think *I'm* blunt." She was hurt, sure, but she was angry, too. She'd thought they'd found a new connection last night. Now it was as if he was setting fire to the bridge linking them. "Why are you so cold? I told you I wasn't looking for a proposal or a proclamation of undying love…"

"Yet," he bit off.

"Excuse me?" She choked out a laugh and didn't know whether she was surprised or insulted.

He sighed. "Terri, if we keep doing this, it's only going to get more complicated."

Nodding to herself, she asked, "And complications are bad?"

"They are for us," he snapped, irritation sparking around him like a firework show run amok. "We're already trying to figure out this business partner thing and if it's going to work."

"I thought it was working," she said and felt the flush of pleasure she'd experienced at the meeting slowly drain away. "You liked my ideas. Ethan and Sharon both discovered they'd work. We're moving forward on them…"

He pushed one hand through his hair, then took hold of her upper arms, pulling her in close. Terri tipped her head back to look up at him and didn't feel any better when she met his gaze.

"You had a couple of good ideas, yeah. And I'm not

taking anything away from you. But Terri, running this company is more than that. And I don't know that you're ready for it."

She'd been feeling pretty confident about it all until just now. "Well, we can't know until I try."

"Trying might cost us too much."

"Again. Won't know until we try."

"And the complications be damned?"

"They're only complications if we allow them to be." Deliberately, she ignored the ice in his eyes and the rigid tension in his body. Going up on her toes, she slanted her mouth over his and it took less than five seconds for him to kiss her back. To wrap his arms around her, hold her tightly to him and devour her mouth with all the passion they'd shared the night before.

Her heart leaped into a gallop and her blood simmered into a fast boil. Would it always feel like this when he touched her? Kissed her? She really wanted to know the answer. Would they be simply business partners? Or lovers as well? When Terri finally pulled back, breaking the kiss, she looked up into his eyes and smiled. "So I'll see you later?"

He took a breath and nodded and she saw heat in his eyes again. "Yeah. You will."

Dave wasn't happy.

Everyone in that meeting had come out singing Terri's praises. How could it have come to this? She was supposed to be a fish out of water here. Supposed to be embarrassing herself and irritating everyone

who worked with her. Instead, she was the golden girl. She'd talked the head chef out of quitting when he was furious with a sous-chef. She'd promoted Debra in reservations to assistant manager. And the rest of the employees were deliriously happy at their newly instated right to switch shifts on their own. How was she doing all of this?

And even if she had made some inroads in this one hotel and casino, what the hell did a bank teller from Utah know about running a multibillion-dollar company? Why were they letting her make suggestions on expansion? And how the hell had she come up with a winning idea?

Somehow, she'd managed to pull off what everyone was saying was the next big thing. *Luxury hotels for families?* Hayes was going to be catering to kids now? And they thought that was *good*? Plus, what was this crap about a coffee setup in the rooms? Since when was that a great idea? Hell, she'd had Cooper moving on that one so fast, Dave heard that housekeeping was scrambling to buy up every damn hot pot in Vegas.

She was entrenching herself in the Hayes Corporation.

Digging in deeper with Cooper himself.

Dave's future was disappearing in front of his eyes.

He had to get rid of her. Fast.

Terri saw the picture on the internet as soon as she got back to her office. She and Celeste, crossing the little stone bridge outside the Venetian. And the head-

line read, *Ex-lover and current lover of Cooper Hayes. Comparing notes?*

"Oh, God." Terri slumped in her chair. Celeste might be used to having her privacy compromised, but Terri wasn't. "What's next? I'm giving birth to alien babies?" She grabbed her phone and called her mother.

"Well, hi, sweetie," her mom said. "If you're calling about the picture, yes, I saw it."

Of course she'd seen it. The Celebrity Watcher missed nothing.

"This is so embarrassing," Terri muttered and thought about her friends and neighbors in Utah seeing the same headline. Closing her eyes, she imagined Jan's reaction and could almost hear her friend laughing hysterically.

"Why are you embarrassed?" her mother asked. "You're a grown woman. You're allowed to have a lover—as long as he's not married, involved or pining away for someone else."

"He's not." Well, not the first two, anyway. Terri really couldn't be sure he didn't still have some feelings for Celeste. What man wouldn't? And she was the one who'd walked away from him. But if he still cared, he was hiding it well.

"Then there's no problem. How's everything else, honey?"

"Crazy, but better, I think." Cooper still had doubts, but Terri was on her way to proving herself. To him. To everyone.

When she'd first arrived in Las Vegas, she'd felt overwhelmed and unsure of herself. But she was learn-

ing the job, the company. She was making friends and fitting into this new life a lot easier than she'd thought she would when she arrived. But most important, Terri was learning that she wanted this more than she'd expected to. Meeting the employees, making sure their guests were happy, it was all...fun. And isn't that what work should be?.

"It sounds to me like you've made up your mind about this new life," her mother said a little wistfully. "You like it, don't you?"

"I do. And before you ask, it's not just Cooper," she said, "though I admit, he's a big part of it all. But I like the challenge, Mom. I love knowing that I can have an idea that will change the way we do things."

"*We*. That's a statement right there."

"Yeah, I guess it is. Am I crazy to decide to change my whole life after hardly a couple of weeks?"

"Sweetie, you've never been crazy. Your aunt Connie, *she's* crazy."

Terri laughed as her mother had meant her to.

"You're a smart, capable woman, Terri. You know what you want and when you make a decision, it's the right one for you."

"Thanks, Mom and oh, I promise to come and collect Daisy soon."

"Daisy's fine, don't worry about that." She paused, then said, "I just poured myself a glass of wine and got down a bag of chips. Tell me everything."

While Terri talked, her mind was working. Now that her decision was made, she'd have to go back to Utah

and put her house up for sale. If she was going to commit to this life, then she was going all in.

Over the next week Terri threw herself into her new life. She had meetings with Sharon and Ethan about the new London hotel, which would be in Kensington. They'd found the perfect property—a beautiful old hotel that desperately needed some loving attention. Once it was purchased, they'd start the renovations, and the hope was to have the first Hayes 2 open for business by next summer.

She'd also spent a lot of time working with housekeeping and hospitality on the tea and coffee services. With a selection of herbal and caffeinated teas, not to mention cookies, granola bars and biscuits, the feedback from their guests was overwhelmingly positive. And to soothe Eli's worries, the coffee station in the lobby *and* room service were reporting that people were still ordering their coffees and breakfasts.

Every day brought a new challenge that she was happy to meet. Between working with the bartenders to devise a way to shift-change that wouldn't inconvenience anyone, and helping out at registration when one of the clerks had to go home sick, Terri was busy—and enjoying herself far more than she once had on the teller line at the bank.

And every night, she was with Cooper. Her heart was happy, but her mind kept warning her about possible problems. Cooper was still holding a part of himself back from her, though it did feel as though she was chipping away at his emotional walls bit by bit.

It was important. She had to make him realize that there was more between them than heat. She had to find a way to let him know she was falling in love with him. Not something she'd planned on, but how could she help it? He was sexy and kind and warm and standoffish and altogether a man who would keep her intrigued and attracted forever. She liked the way his mind worked. She liked the flash of respect for her she saw in his eyes.

And she knew it wouldn't take much for her to finish that beautiful slide into a love so deep and rich that it would kill her if she lost it.

All she had to do was prove to him that she was here to stay. Then he'd be able to drop the shields surrounding his heart and see what she already did. That they made a great team.

So late one afternoon, when Dave came to her with an opportunity, she grabbed it.

"He's an elusive investor," Dave said as he took the elevator with her down to the StarBar for a private meeting. "Honestly, Cooper's been trying to convince the man to invest in Hayes Corporation for years. If you could pull this off, it would completely convince Cooper that you can do this job."

Terri gave him a quick hug. "Thanks, Dave. I appreciate your confidence in me."

"You've earned it," Dave said with a quick grin. "Just convince Simon you're interested and the rest will take care of itself."

"I can do that." And once she did, it would prove

to Cooper once and for all that she was serious about being a part of StarFire. That she could be the partner he needed—not just in the business, but in his life. And once he relaxed about all of it, she could tell him that she was falling in love with him. Terri slapped one hand to her belly at the swirl of nerves nestled there. Dave didn't notice the sudden shock she felt, thank God. *Love.* Funny how that one word could color everything around you. She saw Dave's loyalty. Celeste's friendship. This hotel and the employees who were becoming her friends. She saw the business started by a father she'd never known but who had trusted her with what he'd built.

Mostly, though, she saw Cooper.

The man who had swept her off her feet right from the first. He was icy and warm, cut off and vulnerable. He was all business and then tender. He was, in short, everything she wanted. And maybe, Terri told herself, she'd loved him all along. Or maybe it had awakened in the middle of the night when she woke to find herself in the circle of his arms. But it didn't really matter *when* she began to love him. It was enough to know that she did and she always would.

Dave winked. "I know you can do it."

Terri was going to make sure of it.

By the time Terri finished her meeting with Simon Baxter of TravelOn and got back up to the offices to tell Cooper all about it, most everyone on the business floor had gone home for the day. The desks were empty and her footsteps echoed in the silence. The

quiet in the normally busy room was so absolute, it was a little spooky.

But that unsettled feeling disappeared when she opened Cooper's door and saw him sitting at his desk. Through the window behind him, the soft glow of neon shone against the glass. Cooper's jacket was off, tie loosened and the top collar button of his shirt undone.

The love she'd only just acknowledged filled her heart and spilled over into warmth that slid through her bloodstream. How could she not have recognized what she felt for Cooper before now? Because they hadn't known each other very long? What did time have to do with anything? Her adoptive parents had fallen in love over a weekend, gotten married three weeks later and had had forty-two years together before her dad died.

And she wanted that with Cooper. Wanted this life she'd just discovered. Wanted him. Wanted the family they could build together. Just looking at him made her heart race. Then he looked up and the smile that flashed briefly across his face when he saw her, left Terri pretty much a goner. Love rose up inside her and opened like a spring tulip. It was lovely and so necessary, she didn't know how she'd lived this long without it.

Now she would show him that she loved him. That they were great together. That she could be his partner, personally and in business. Even though the office was empty, she closed his door behind her, wanting to ensure their privacy.

"Hi," he said. "I was just going to head upstairs. Where've you been?"

"I was at a meeting," she said, walking toward him.

Frowning a little, he pulled her down onto his lap. "With who?"

"That's the surprise," she said, squirming around on his lap until she could face him. Wrapping her arms around his neck, she leaned in and kissed him hard. Excitement was still fluttering inside her. She'd done it. She'd struck a deal with Simon and now all it needed was Cooper's approval. Terri couldn't wait to see his face when she told him.

"I was talking with Simon Baxter."

"What?"

She grinned at the shock in his eyes. And it was about to get even better. "Simon has agreed to invest in Hayes Corporation. I think it's a really good deal, but of course, none of it will go forward until I get your agreement."

"My *agreement*?" He pulled her arms down from his neck and stared at her as if he'd never seen her before. "What the hell did you do?"

Confused, Terri just blinked at him. "I told you. I talked to Simon and we agreed on an investment level. But Cooper, nothing's set in stone until you approve it, too."

"And I never will." He lifted her off his lap, set her on her feet, then jumped out of his chair as if he couldn't stay still a moment longer. "Why would you do that?"

Terri didn't understand why he was so furious, but

he definitely was. His eyes were flashing, his jaw was tight and he practically vibrated with outrage.

"He's an investor," she said. "I thought that was a good thing."

"If it was, I'd have taken him up on his offer ten years ago when I lost my dad." Jamming both hands through his hair, he shook his head. "Simon Baxter, the motel king. God. I can't believe you went behind my back on this."

"I didn't go behind your back, Cooper." Terri was stunned. He was looking at her as if she'd stabbed him through the heart. How had this all gone so wrong so quickly?

"That's what it looks like from here," he countered and walked away from her as if needing the distance. "I don't *want* outside investors, Terri. Never have. Hell, I didn't want *you.*"

Shock punched her and she watched him through eyes suddenly blurred by unexpected tears. She blinked frantically. Damned if she'd cry.

"This is *my* company, Terri," he raged. "I'm the one who took it over from my dad and built it up into what it is now. And I did it without anyone's help."

"What about my father? What about Jacob?" she countered. "He was your partner. You weren't all alone in this, Cooper."

"Jacob came in and out, but he didn't stick his nose into the running of the business. Which is more than I can say for *you*. The running of the company, the building it into what it is now? That was me. I did it my

damn self." He paused, jerked his head back and gave her a hard look. "Is this why you really came here?"

He started pacing in long, fast strides. "Have you been playing me all along? Setting me up for a take-over? You're all innocence and sex, getting past my guard, easing me into a situation that you set up? How the hell much is Simon promising you to betray me?"

"Betray?" She took a step toward him and stopped. "I only did this as a surprise for you."

He laughed shortly but there was no amusement in the sound. "Surprise? Well, congratulations. You pulled it off. I thought you didn't play games."

"Play games? I *don't*." How had it come to this? Why was she defending herself to a man who had al-ready tried and convicted her? "Aren't you the one who keeps telling me that there's no BS with me? That I'm blunt? To the point?"

She didn't know why he was so angry, but she hadn't done anything to be ashamed of. She'd only talked to Simon with the best of intentions. "Now all of a sudden you think I'm scheming? Well, you're *wrong*."

He snorted. "Of course you'd say that."

"Well yeah, because it's *true*." Terri shook her head and tried to figure out where she'd zigged when she should have zagged.

Maybe she should have talked to Cooper about the meeting first, but Dave had assured her this was some-thing Cooper wanted. And when that thought settled in her mind, she began to wonder if it wasn't someone else pulling the strings here. Was it Dave, leading her

into this very confrontation for reasons of his own? She'd trusted him. *Cooper* trusted him.

"I don't play games, Cooper. I don't lie. And I wasn't working against you. I was trying to do this *for* you."

He snorted again. She was really getting tired of that sound.

She took a breath and tried again. "I'd never even heard of Simon Baxter until Dave told me he was here and wanted to meet."

"Dave?" His head whipped up and his cold, cold eyes met hers.

"Yes," she insisted. She had to make him understand that she never would have done anything to hurt him. "Dave told me that you'd be happy about this. That I could finally prove to you that I can be your partner. That's the only reason I went to the meeting in the first place."

Seconds ticked past quietly while he stared at her. Terri felt sick that it had come to this. She hated seeing the repulsed look in his eyes but couldn't think of a way to get past it.

Finally, he spoke. "You expect me to believe that my oldest friend is the one who turned on me? Dave and I have worked together for more than ten years. You've been here a few weeks. I'm supposed to take your word over his?"

Her chest hurt. Her eyes stung. Her breath was like knives moving in and out of her lungs. She wouldn't have believed it possible for everything in her life to turn so quickly to trash. But the look in Cooper's eyes

told the story. He didn't believe her. He'd even said out loud that he hadn't even *wanted* her there.

"So you'd rather believe it was me, is that it?"

"I didn't say that."

"You didn't have to. I don't care who you believe, Cooper," she said, voice tight, but steady. She did care, of course. Desperately. But she wouldn't give him the satisfaction of seeing how much his words had torn at her. "But if you think so little of me, after all we've shared, then I have to wonder if you're the one who's been playing me all this time."

When he didn't say anything, just kept looking at her with those icy-blue eyes, Terri sighed and felt her soul shrivel into a ball of pain. "You have, haven't you?"

He shifted his gaze away from hers. "No."

"Don't lie to me," she murmured, waiting for him to look at her again. "You kept waiting for me to fail. You *wanted* me to fail so I'd leave and you could have your precious company all to yourself again."

"Terri…" He ground his teeth together and scowled tightly. But he didn't deny a thing.

"Congratulations. I never saw it. Didn't even consider you were just biding your time before buying me out. It must have been really frustrating for you when I succeeded."

"Damn it, Terri—"

"Don't curse at me, either." She took a breath, squared her shoulders and lifted her chin. Her gaze burned into his as she said, "I didn't fail, Cooper. *You* did."

She turned to leave but stopped when he spoke again.

"Got another meeting?" Cooper taunted.

"No." She looked back at him, the man she loved. The man who didn't trust her. Didn't want her. "I just don't want to be here anymore."

Ten

In her suite, Terri gave in to the tumult inside and allowed the first tears to fall. She couldn't believe what had happened. Why had Dave done that to her? Why would he deliberately set her up? Had Cooper's reaction been an act? Had he and Dave done this together?

"No," she muttered. "He wasn't acting. He was surprised. Furious."

She dropped her black bag on the long, slim dining table and only then noticed a brown envelope with her name typed efficiently on the front. She swiped tears out of her eyes, picked up the envelope and tore it open. With her luck it would be an eviction notice signed by Cooper himself.

Sniffing, she sat down at the dining table and pulled the papers free. First, there was a typewritten letter

from Mr. Seaton, Jacob Evans's lawyer. The man who'd come to see her in Ogden and started all of this.

Ms. Ferguson, as per your late father's wishes, this letter from him is delivered three weeks following his death.

A letter. From the father she would never know. Terri was almost afraid to read it. With everything else going on right now, could she take one more buffeting? But even as she considered ignoring it, she unfolded the letter and read...

My dear Terri,

Though I've not been a part of your life, I have kept a fatherly, if distant, eye on you all these years. Your parents were good people and I am grateful to them for loving you the way I couldn't.

But I want you to know that your mother and I were very young and very much in love. She became pregnant and we made plans to run away together after your birth. But I lost my love the night you were born. She died and you lived. I knew that alone, I couldn't give you the life you deserved, so I allowed your adoption. It was the hardest thing I have ever done.

Terri's eyes filled with tears that spilled over and ran, unheeded, down her cheeks.

I want you to know that you were loved even before you were born.

And though you rightly loved your parents, I hope that sometimes, you might spare a thought for the parents who loved you and let you go.

Be happy, Terri.
Your father,
Jacob Evans.

Terri's tears blurred the page as she carefully folded it again. Too many emotions in one night, she thought as her throat closed up with a wave of sympathy, regret and loss rising up to settle in the center of her chest.

"It's too much," she whispered. "All of it. I feel like I can't breathe." She looked around the lavish suite— four thousand square feet of emptiness—and felt as barren as the room in which she sat. She needed comfort. So she stood up, walked to the closest phone and dialed room service.

"Hi," she said, hoping she didn't sound as pitiful as she felt. "I need you to send up the biggest hot fudge sundae we have. And a slice of chocolate cake. Twenty minutes? That's great. Thank you."

While she waited, she opened a bottle of white wine, poured herself a glass and muttered, "Wine and chocolate. Perfect."

Jacob Evans had loved her. She'd never know him.

Terri loved Cooper Hayes. She'd never have him.

Her heart was torn, her insides felt as if they'd been sliced to ribbons and the flush of success she'd been feeling only hours ago had completely dissipated.

"He hadn't wanted me to succeed. That's why he

kept looking surprised at everything I did." Shaking her head, she sat down at the dining table, dug into her purse and pulled out her cell phone. "I need a friend. A *real* friend." And there was only one person who came to mind.

Texting her, she wrote:

Can you take some sick days starting tomorrow? I need the cavalry.

Sure. What's wrong? What happened?
What do you need?

Terri grinned. God, it was good to have someone you could count on no matter what.

I'll tell all when you get here. Buying you a ticket, will email it to you.

Okay, bazillionaire, I'll let you.

Terri laughed and it sounded broken, even to her.

Thanks, Jan.

Just tell me who you want me to slap.
See you tomorrow.

Flipping open the laptop on the table, Terri hurriedly checked into Jan's favorite airline's site, bought a ticket for first thing in the morning, then emailed it to her.

Then she sat back, took another sip of wine and swallowed past the knot of emotion lodged in her throat. Terri felt lost. It was as if everything she'd believed since coming here had all been a lie. Had she ever really had a shot at this? Or had it all been a play acted out by really convincing actors?

A knock on the door sounded and she opened it to room service. The young guy carried a tray holding a gigantic sundae and the biggest slice of chocolate cake she'd ever seen.

"Anything else, Ms. Ferguson?"

"No," she said, handing him a ten dollar tip. "That's it, Rory. Thank you."

"Yes, ma'am."

She winced, but laughed as she locked the door. Funny, now being called ma'am was the least of her problems.

By morning Cooper was ready to kick some ass.

All night long he'd been awake, thinking about the confrontation with Terri. What he'd said to her. What Terri had said back. The look on her face when he'd accused her of betraying him. He couldn't forget it. The pain in her eyes. The way her mouth had dropped open in complete shock. She'd folded her arms over her middle as if in a futile attempt to shield herself from more verbal attacks. *He'd* done that to her.

Shaking his head, he dismissed her response as irrelevant. He couldn't worry about her hurt feelings when the rug had just been pulled out from beneath his feet.

Terri turning on him was one thing. Hell, until her he'd never really known a woman he could learn to trust. But to know that it was Dave—his best friend—the one man he had always trusted over all others, who was behind it all, was too much to swallow.

Naturally, he hadn't taken Terri's word for a damn thing. He'd told himself that she was covering up, trying to make herself appear innocent while tossing Dave to the dogs. So Cooper had done the only thing he could to try to get to the truth. He'd called Simon Baxter. Just remembering that brief conversation ripped him open again.

Maybe he should have believed Terri. She'd always been nothing but honest with him. He'd held himself back from her to protect himself and in doing so had really screwed everything up. But who could blame him for not wanting to admit that it was his oldest friend who had betrayed him.

"Simon," he'd said, clenching the phone to his ear while he stalked up and down the balcony at his end of the owner's floor. He avoided even looking at the French doors to Terri's suite. "I hear you had an investment meeting tonight with my new partner."

Keep it friendly, open. Get him to spill what he knew.

"I did," Simon confirmed jovially. "That's a smart young woman you've got there, Hayes. She drives a tough bargain. Yes, you're a lucky man."

"Yeah. Sure I am." He felt as lucky as a man climbing the steps to his own gallows, but that was beside the

point at the moment. "Terri tells me it was really Dave who got the ball rolling this time around."

In the background, Cooper heard the click of a lighter and knew the older man was lighting up one of his beloved cigars. Celebrating what he thought was a coup?

"That's right," Simon said. "Ol' Dave has been assuring me for a year now that you'd come around eventually. See the sense in us joining forces."

Cooper's heart sank even as his fury roared into life. It was a struggle to keep his voice steady. "Is that so?"

"Well, hell, you know that boy is really ambitious—got yourself a live wire there, Hayes. But he's loyal to you. Got your best interests at heart. He sees that the two of us merging would be good for both our houses."

Sure. Because a five-star hotel company merging with a roadside motel outfit couldn't be anything but great. What the hell had Dave been thinking? A year? A year, he'd been working on this behind Cooper's back? What the hell else had he been up to?

Cooper had gotten what he needed, so he wrapped it up.

"Well, Simon, I hate to disappoint you again," he said tightly. "But my company's going to stay privately held. No outside investments. No mergers."

"Well, here now, that's not what Dave's been feeding me for a damn year. It's not what that girl had to say last night, either!" Outrage colored the older man's voice but he had nothing on how Cooper was feeling.

"Dave doesn't have the power to make deals, Simon. You know that. As for Terri," he muttered, rubbing one

hand across his forehead as if to ease the ache pounding there. A cold wind slapped at him and it felt as if the universe itself was trying to push him around. "She's new here and doesn't understand." Though apparently, she'd understood Dave in a way Cooper hadn't. What was he supposed to make of that?

"Dave said this was all for you. That you'd okayed it."

"He lied." God, those words tasted bitter. But damn if he didn't have to swallow them. His friend had betrayed him. Tried to sell him out. Working deals and using Terri to do it.

"Now, see here," Simon blustered.

"We're done, Simon," Cooper said and hung up. It took all his control not to throw his damn cell phone against the wall just to watch it shatter.

Terri has been telling the truth. But did that change anything, really? She was still the partner he hadn't wanted. She'd done some good work in the last couple of weeks, had come up with some fresh ideas that were already panning out. But she still didn't belong, did she? Even as he thought it, he told himself that of course she did. She'd proven herself there to him. To all of them.

And he'd never wanted a damn partner, so why should he be expected to just welcome her with open arms? If she stayed, they'd get drawn deeper and deeper into what had already grown into something far more than temporary. Was he ready for that? Hell, was he even capable of it?

Shoving the memory of that phone call and the long,

lonely, miserable night that followed to the back of his mind, Cooper stood up when Dave knocked, then walked into the room with all of his usual, casual flair.

"Come on in."

Grinning, Dave said, "You wanted to see me?"

"Yeah." Cooper came around his desk, perched on the edge of it and watched his friend come closer. More than ten years they'd worked together, played together, had each other's backs—or so Cooper had thought. Now he had to wonder if Dave had been working against him all along. How much of their relationship had been a lie right from the beginning?

"Terri told me she met with Simon Baxter last night."

Wincing, Dave shrugged. "Yeah, she told me she wanted to meet him. I didn't want to introduce them, Cooper." He lifted both hands in a helpless shrug. "But she *is* a partner here so I didn't feel I could refuse."

Clearly, Dave was going to ride this horse right into the ground. Nodding, Cooper said, "Plus, it would have been hard to refuse when you're the one who set it all up to begin with."

"What?" He laughed, but the sound was nervous.

"You've been working for a year to get something going with Simon," Cooper continued, watching his friend's eyes, seeing the flash of guilt before it disappeared again.

"Oh, come on. Really?"

Ignoring the halfhearted denials, Cooper asked, "If Jacob hadn't died—if Terri hadn't shown up—how were you going to work it?"

"Are you nuts?"

"No. I'm pissed." Cooper saw it in his eyes. Dave was realizing that there was no point in denying anything anymore. "How the hell could you do this, Dave? We're *friends*. We've worked together for years."

"Together?" Dave choked out a laugh and shook his head. "No, Cooper, you're my *boss*. I work for you."

"So the hell what?" Stunned, confused, Cooper countered, "You're my assistant. That's a bad thing?"

"You still don't get it." He laughed again. "A bad thing? I hate every minute of it." Every semblance of a smile, of friendship, drained from his expression and his eyes were fiery. "Everything about it. I jump when you say, go where you say, do what you say. My God, I do most of the damn work around here and I'm still just an employee. I'll never be *more*."

"If you believe all of that, you're the one who's nuts. Yeah, you do a good job, but we all do." Outraged, Cooper said, "Oh and yeah. Poor you. Sorry about the six-figure salary and the five weeks of vacation every year—at whatever Hayes hotel you want to stay in. Yeah, it's rough to be you."

Dave sneered at him. "What the hell do you know about anything? You're the golden boy. Everything goes your way. You've got money falling out of your pockets. Your ex charges a ten thousand dollar dress to your account and you shrug it off as a cheap way to keep her occupied.

"You want to know how I would have handled Simon if that *simpleton* hadn't shown up to take over? I'd have gotten the shares you promised me and I'd

have sold them all to Simon for a damn fortune. Then *finally*, I could have lived the way I want to. Hell. The way I deserve to."

The viciousness pouring out of the man shook Cooper. How could he not have seen any of this in all this time? Hell, he'd never even guessed that Dave was so eaten up by jealousy that it had soured him completely. Ten years with this man and it turned out Cooper didn't know him at all. What did that say about his judgment? He wanted to trust Terri but how the hell could he let himself? What if the face Terri showed him was as false as the one Dave had been wearing for years?

"Man, you should be an actor. You kept up the best friend role all these years and never let a damn thing slip."

"Please." Dave waved one hand. "You see what you want to see. Always have. God, you looked at Terri and saw a mastermind trying to sell you out?" He laughed. "Seriously? *Her?*"

"She's no simpleton," Cooper said tightly. "In the short time she's been here, she's turned quite a few things around. Plus, she's not a liar. That's something you wouldn't understand."

"Really? And you do?" Dave sneered and shook his head. "Didn't you just chase her off, accusing her of backstabbing you?"

He had. Pain jabbed at him at the reminder of how she'd looked at him. How she'd turned and walked away. How he hadn't stopped her. And he'd deal with the guilt of that later. For now, though… "Time for you to go, Dave."

"Oh, I'm going. Don't worry. I'll be hired at another hotel chain before the week's out."

"I wish them luck." Cooper folded his arms across his chest. "We were friends once, so I won't have you tossed out…"

Dave held up one hand. "Spare me the speeches."

"Fine. No speech. Just two more words. You're fired."

Even after this confrontation, Cooper could see that the finality of those words slapped at Dave. But he recovered quickly. "Fine. I'll take my severance package in lieu of notice. And I won't miss any of this one damn bit."

When he left, Cooper stared at the door for a long time, wondering if Dave was right about at least one thing. Did Cooper only see what he wanted to? Was he blind to anything that might shake up his view of the world?

Okay, two things. He *had* assumed that Terri was the betrayer. Even knowing her inherent honesty and the fact that she could be as blunt as a sledgehammer, he'd believed it. Or at least a part of him had.

Because it was easier that way. It would have given him an excuse to get rid of her. To buy her out and make her leave. It would have given him a reason to stop this connection with her before his feelings grew even more than they already had.

And now that the damage was done, the question was, did he try to undo it? Or did he leave it alone for both their sakes? He wanted to go to her. To hold her, tell her he was wrong. Tell her that what he felt for her

was so damn startling he didn't know what to do with it. But he didn't. Because if she left now, he didn't want to watch her go.

Terri opened the door and Jan rushed in. Her short, spiky black hair was perfect and her bright green eyes sparkled. She wore black leggings, a sapphire-blue tunic sweater and flat black boots.

"Wow! First class plane ticket, a limo with champagne to pick me up and a gorgeous bellman to wheel my bag. I could get used to this." Jan dropped her purse onto the dining table and pulled Terri into a hug.

Terri hugged her back, more relieved than she could say that Jan, with her outsized personality and fierce loyalty, was there with her. Then she looked past her friend and saw Jake, the bellman, waiting.

"Oh, hey," Jan turned and reached for her purse. "I need to tip you and—"

"No, you don't," Jake said with a wink and a wicked grin. "It's on the house."

When he left, Jan fanned herself. "Boy, he's a cutie, huh?" When she looked at Terri, Jan must have read the misery on her friend's face because she instantly went feral. "Okay, who hurt you? Just point me at them."

"God, it's good to see you," Terri said softly. "Everything's just a mess."

"Messes can be cleaned up," Jan told her and threaded her arm through Terri's walking into the living room. "Let me have one minute to have a small orgasm over this suite, then you can tell me all about it."

Terri laughed, dropped onto the couch and started

talking. Jan's features displayed every emotion in the book as Terri went through what had been happening in the past couple of weeks. She told her everything, didn't hold back, and by the time she was finished, Jan was furious.

"What is the matter with this Cooper? Can't he see you were set up?"

"I don't know," Terri said, still hurt from the night before. "Maybe he doesn't want to know it. He said himself he never wanted me here."

Jan gave her a gentle shove. "Well, it wasn't up to him, was it?"

"No, but maybe it is now."

"Why?" Irritated, Jan jumped to her feet, walked away a few steps, then came right back. "You're a partner in this business, Terri. He doesn't have the right to bitch about it. Well, okay, he can bitch, but he can't change it."

"No, but I can," Terri admitted. Leading the way over to the wet bar, she opened the fridge, pulled out a bottle of wine and uncorked it. As she poured two glasses, she said, "I wanted you to come because I needed the company on my drive back to Ogden."

"What?" Jan took her glass and had a sip.

"I want to stop by my mom's and pick up Daisy, but then I'm going back home. I don't belong here, Jan. And Cooper doesn't *want* me here."

"So you quit?" Jan set her glass down, propped both hands on her hips and gave Terri a hard look. "Really? Your birth father wanted you to have what he spent a lifetime achieving and you're going to walk away be-

cause Cooper's bent out of shape? You came here for you, remember? Because it was finally your time to do something that you wanted to do."

Put like that, leaving, giving up, sounded like a terrible idea. But Terri had been haunted all night by these and a million other thoughts. And alone in the dark, she'd decided that this was the best way. Just leave the situation. Let Cooper have his business. She'd proven to him and to herself that she was up to the task. That she could do anything. Maybe that was enough.

"It's easier this way," she argued. "I sell him my shares and we never have to see each other again."

"Uh-huh." Jan shook her head and dropped into one of the chairs, waving a hand at Terri to get her to do the same. "And the fact that you love him is what— going to be ignored?"

"It has to be. He doesn't want me here, Jan."

"Because you're dangerous to him, Terri."

She laughed. "Me? Dangerous?"

"Yeah, you." Jan took a breath and let it out again. "He's had everything his own way for so long, he doesn't know how to share."

"He's not a kindergartner," Terri said.

"*All* men are kindergartners," Jan countered.

"So I should stay and be miserable waiting for him to come to his senses?" Terri shook her head firmly. "That doesn't sound like a good time to me."

"Well, hell, of course not," Jan said. "But why should you be miserable? You said yourself that until this blowup with Cooper, you were having a great time. You've got a knack for this and you know it." Terri's.

"You have just as much right to be here as Cooper, yes?"

"Yeah…"

"You've come up with a few great ideas already, right?"

"True, but—"

"You've got friends here, don't you?"

"I don't know," Terri admitted, thinking about all of the people she'd met and worked with over the past couple of weeks. Yesterday, she would have said she did have friends. She would have counted Dave among them. Now how could she be sure about any of them?

"Well, I do. You're *you*, Terri. You've got friends. People who are on your side. Are you really going to walk away? Show them all that you can be defeated this easily?"

"Easy?"

"Okay, bad word, but you know what I mean." Jan gave her hand a squeeze and sat back. "Don't give it up, Terri. Don't let him take this from you. You wanted this. For yourself. Why should you leave because he's being a giant pain in the ass?"

Jan had a point. Heck, she had *lots* of points. Terri felt her balance reassert itself. Jan was right. About a lot of things. And this is exactly why Terri had needed to talk to Jan. Her friend saw through layers to the bottom line better than anyone she'd ever known. And she knew she could trust Jan. With anything. Terri only wished that Jan were here all the time instead of all the way in Ogden… Terri actually *felt* the lightbulb go off in her head as a brilliant idea occurred to her.

"I'll stay," she said quietly. "I've made something here. Something I love. That I'm good at. You're right. I shouldn't have to leave to make Cooper feel better, so I'll stay."

"Atta girl!" Jan grinned, toasted her with the wine and took a big gulp.

"If you will," Terri finished.

"What?" Confused, Jan looked at her and waited.

"How would you like to move to Vegas and work at Hayes Corporation as my executive assistant?"

"Are you serious?" Jan asked, her eyes flashing excitement.

"Oh, yeah. Very serious. I really need you here, Jan. I can trust you to always be honest with me. To tell me when I'm being stupid or about to make a huge mistake—to come up with fabulous ideas to shake up both the company and Cooper—" The more she said, the more Terri knew this was the right thing to do. She could have her best friend with her, and Jan would be making more than twice as much as she had in Ogden.

"Well, sure, but you don't have to *hire* me for that."

"Just hear me out," Terri said quickly and this time it was she reaching for her friend's hand. "You can live here with me. This suite is four thousand square feet."

"Holy God!" Jan's gaze whipped around the room, then back to Terri. "That's bigger than both our condos put together!"

"I know! We'll have plenty of room. And you'd work for me. I'll pay you a huge salary and you'll get great vacations in any of our hotels every year and—"

"Stop the sales pitch," Jan said, scrambling up to

rush around the table. "You had me as soon as you said you needed me. I really missed you the past couple of weeks, Terri. And I'd love to live here. Hello? Jake the bellman for one…"

Terri gave her a tight hug and for the first time since she came to Vegas she felt good about facing the future. Even if that meant working with a man who didn't trust her—and would never love her.

Eleven

God, it was good to laugh again. After an hour with Jan, Terri felt better than she had in a long time. It was going to be brilliant, having Jan in Vegas with her, working with her.

When a knock on her door sounded, Terri's laughter ended abruptly and she had a wild thought that maybe it was Cooper, coming to apologize. To tell her that he'd been wrong from the beginning and that he understood now that he loved her and trusted her and—

"Wow," she muttered, pushing up from the couch. "I lead a rich and full fantasy life."

"Cool," Jan said with a grin. "When you get back, tell me all about it."

"I don't think so," Terri said. Her tiny, hopeless fan-

tasies were better off staying private. Then she looked through the peephole and felt fury rise up inside her.

Yanking the door open, she looked at Dave and demanded, "What're you doing here?"

All apology, Dave squeezed past her before she could close the door on him and shut him out. Holding up both hands, he said, "Just listen to me for a minute, Terri, then I'll go."

She closed the door, crossed her arms over her chest and stood hipshot, tapping the toe of one boot against the tile floor. Behind her, she felt more than heard Jan walk up to join them.

"Who are you?" Dave asked.

"Is this Dave?" Jan asked.

"Yes, this is him. What do you want, Dave? Haven't you already done more than enough?"

Jan lined up beside her and mimicked Terri's stance. "Why are you listening to him, Terri? Let's just toss his ass out."

"Now, just a minute," he argued, flashing a furious glance at Jan.

"No, you wait," Terri interrupted and stepped into his space. Poking him in the chest with her index finger, she demanded, "Why did you do it, Dave? Why did you set me up? Let me think Cooper wanted a merger with Simon Baxter?"

His gaze shifted between Jan and Terri like a cornered dog, before settling on Terri. "It wasn't my idea."

"Really…" Jan wasn't asking a question.

He huffed out an impatient breath and ignored Jan completely. "Terri, Cooper wanted me to do that. He

set it all up so you'd fail miserably. He wanted an excuse to finally get rid of you."

"Bastard," Jan murmured.

Terri had to agree. If it was true.

But she remembered the look of shock and anger on Cooper's face and she was willing to bet it had been real. If he'd been acting, he deserved an award. Shaking her head so hard, her blond ponytail swung from side to side behind her, she said, "That makes no sense at all."

"Sure it does," Dave argued quickly. "He figured you'd be so upset at your 'mistake' that you'd sell him your shares and he'd have what he always wanted. The company all in his name."

"What a crappy thing to do," Jan said.

Terri could feel her friend's anger, but she still wasn't convinced. Not entirely, anyway. "Why are you telling me this? If you were willing to set me up for Cooper's sake, why turn on him now?"

"Because he fired me," Dave said and lifted his chin. "He doesn't want any loose ends. Didn't want to risk you finding out he's been using you all along. For the past couple of weeks, he's been softening you up, placating you by accepting your ideas, sleeping with you to keep you off balance—all to eventually convince you to leave."

Terri felt cold all over. Funny, but anger could be ice as well as fire. Was Cooper really that underhanded and vicious? Or was Dave playing her again for his own reasons? How could she know? She'd cried enough. She'd been furious. Now she was just cold and calm. Cooper had gone through a lot to get rid of her. Why?

Why not be up front and honest in the first place? Why not just offer to buy her out right from the beginning?

Because, her mind whispered, *he'd known you wouldn't walk away then. It was too new. Too important for you to try. So he let you. Encouraged you. All with the plan of making you quit in the end.*

"He doesn't give a damn about you, Terri," Dave was saying. "Or me, for that matter. We've been best friends since college and he just tossed me out. He's incapable of caring, Terri. Cooper Hayes is an empty shell."

She wouldn't have thought so. But she'd seen a side of Cooper after the Simon blowup that she never had before. And still, she knew a Cooper that Dave didn't. Passionate and warm and funny. He didn't seem empty to her—just…guarded. Cooper had to know that Dave would come running to her to spill his guts, wouldn't he? Why would he be loyal to the man who fired him? So again, Terri was left feeling at sea, not knowing which way to turn or who to believe.

He left shortly after and the quiet in the suite was overwhelming. Terri got herself a bottle of water and took a long drink while Jan watched her as if she were an unexploded bomb. Which was what she felt like. Everything inside her was so tension-filled it was a wonder she hadn't already burst.

"Okay." Jan looked at her. "Do we believe him? I mean yeah, we're already mad at Cooper because he's a jerk. But Dave set you up. Why should we believe him now?"

"Good points," Terri murmured as she thought it all through. Dave could have warned her privately last

night before that meeting with Simon Baxter. He could have confessed the truth about Cooper's plan and then sworn her to secrecy. But he hadn't. So no matter how Dave tried to paint himself, he wasn't a good guy. Terri looked at Jan. "Either Dave's lying or Cooper was last night—and for the past couple of weeks."

"How do we tell?"

"I don't know that we can." Terri was disgusted, disappointed and so damn tired of feeling hurt. Had he really been lying to her all this time? Had she trusted, loved a man who had never intended to care?

"So," her friend finally said, "what's next? What do you want to do?"

What she *wanted* to do was face Cooper. To tell him he'd lost. To tell him that she loved him, but he'd lost that, too. And she would.

But first, "Would you call downstairs, Jan? Get the valets to bring my car around?"

"You're leaving?" Surprise flickered in Jan's eyes. "What happened to you not letting Cooper chase you away? What happened to my great new job?"

"I'm not leaving. Well, not for long. I'm going to find Cooper, and then you and I are driving to St. George to see my mom and pick up my dog."

"Okay..."

"Then we're coming back here." Terri's gaze was clear and sharp. "And we're both going to get to work."

"Wahoo!"

Fifteen minutes later Jan was downstairs and Terri was knocking on the door to Cooper's suite right down

the hall. Mentally, she rehearsed just what she would say to him when he opened it. She would stare him down, tell him that she loved him but was determined to get over it. She'd tell him that she was staying in Vegas, no matter what he did to try to make her leave. She would look into his blue eyes and try not to wish that everything was different. But everything in her mind dried up and blew away when the door swung open to show her that Cooper had already moved on.

Celeste Vega, wearing nothing more than a towel, gave her an awkward smile.

Celeste lifted one hand to her mouth in a dramatic fashion, and used her free hand to hold the thick, navy blue towel to her breasts. "Terri! Oh, this is so embarrassing…"

And well thought out, she added silently. Dave had given her his pass key to Cooper's suite. Celeste's plan had been to surprise Cooper with her naked self—ready and willing to resume the relationship she'd turned from nearly two years ago.

But having Terri catch her here? That was hard. She hated to see the look of stunned hurt on the other woman's face, and regret was a new sensation for Celeste. She was used to taking care of herself, no one else. So why did she feel guilty?

"Celeste?" Terri blinked, shook her head and said, "I was looking for Cooper…"

"This is so uncomfortable," Celeste said, tossing a look toward the hallway over her shoulder as if expecting Cooper to walk into the room any second. She was

in so deep now, she had to keep going. Had to make Terri give up on Cooper so Celeste could have another shot at him, So she steeled herself and said, "He's in the shower, sweetie. I'm just about to join him."

Nodding, Terri said, "I see. Okay. Well." She took a deep breath and tried to hide the pain in her eyes. But Celeste saw it and felt another sharp blade of regret slice her heart.

She'd come to Las Vegas to win Cooper back no matter how she had to do it. But hurting Terri was harder than it should have been. Celeste hadn't expected to care for the other woman. To enjoy the budding friendship that was dying miserably at the moment. But she'd come too far to stop now.

Cooper and Terri were already estranged—Dave had told her that much. This, then, would be the driving wedge that would keep them apart. And that was what Celeste wanted, wasn't it?

Meeting Terri's gaze was the hardest thing Celeste had ever done. She felt terrible. A dog. A snake. A worm. And Terri's simple dignity made her feel even worse.

"I'll go, then," Terri said, "and leave you two alone."

"Terri—" Celeste didn't want her to be hurt. But this is how it had to be. Still, she wanted to say something to ease Terri's pain. What, she had no idea. As it turned out, it didn't matter.

"It's all right, Celeste," Terri said softly. "Cooper's made his choice. Would you tell him that I'm leaving? I'm driving to St. George."

She frowned. "Where is that?"

"In Utah. My mom lives there. So…" She took another breath. "Just tell him, okay?"

Celeste reached out and took Terri's arm as she turned to leave. Her gaze fixed on Terri's, Celeste said, "You really love him, don't you?"

Inhaling sharply, she answered, "Yes. But don't hold it against me. I'm sure I'll get over it."

Cooper was done. He'd been dealing with the fallout of Dave's treachery all day—a couple more of his employees were now looking for jobs thanks to being involved with Dave's plans. Plus, he'd had to handle all the things Terri had taken on.

After last night he wasn't surprised that she wasn't in her office, but he was shocked to realize that she had become so important to the simple running of the business. When had she taken on so much of the day-to-day drivel that went with running a huge company?

"And how the hell does she get anything done with everyone running to her every five minutes with some petty complaint?" He shook his head and looked down the hall toward her suite.

She was in there, no doubt still furious with him, and he really couldn't blame her. He'd been a bastard. Worse, a *blind* bastard. Dave had worked her, Cooper had used her and all she'd done was work her ass off.

"And damn it, I *miss* her." It wasn't just his own busy mind keeping him awake the night before. It was being without her. He'd reached for her countless times and found only an empty bed and cold sheets.

He missed her laugh, the shine in her eyes when

she was excited by something. He missed hearing her stories about what was happening in his own damn casino and mostly, he just missed her. Her smile. Her scent. Her taste. God. Cooper suddenly felt like he'd been hit over the head with a two-by-four.

He *loved* Terri Ferguson. When the hell had that happened?

He didn't want to buy her out. He didn't want her to leave. He wanted her here. With him. His partner. And so much more. So, just exactly how could he fix this?

He unlocked his door, walked into the suite and stopped at the sound of a familiar voice.

"You're late."

Cooper jolted and looked to the couch where Celeste sat, wrapped in one of his bath towels. "Oh, no. Not today. What the hell are you doing here, Celeste?"

"I came to seduce you," she admitted, rising to her feet with the grace of a ballet dancer.

"Thanks, but no, thanks," he ground out. He didn't want her.

He wanted Terri.

Damn it, why hadn't he gone to her earlier?

"I've lost, then, haven't I?" Celeste dropped the towel to the floor.

Cooper got a full frontal look at one of the most beautiful women in the world—his own ex-lover—and didn't feel a thing. All he could think was, *She's not Terri.* He wondered how the hell she'd gotten in, then figured it had to be *Dave.*

Celeste picked up her short black dress from where

she'd tossed it earlier and shimmied into it. Then she backed up to Cooper and said, "Zip?"

He sighed, zipped her dress and took a step back. "Go away, Celeste. Seriously. I'm not in the mood for whatever you're playing."

Turning around to face him, she looked him dead in the eye to say, "Before I go, you should know that Terri was here."

"What?" He grabbed her upper arms. "When?"

"About a half hour ago." She bent down, picked up the towel and handed it to him. "She found me wearing this. I told her you were in the shower, waiting for me to join you."

A hot jolt of anger erupted. At her. At himself for letting it come to this. "Damn you, Celeste. Why the hell would you do that to her? She *likes* you."

"Because I wanted you back," she said, fluffing her hair then smoothing her palms over her hips. "I decided that I could get rid of Terri and have you to myself."

"No, you can't," he said tightly. "What we had is long dead, Celeste. Not interested in a replay."

Her eyebrows arched. "Not kind, but sadly a truth I'm forced to accept. I don't like it. Comfortable lies are so much easier to live with than hard truths.

"Do you know, until I met Terri, I hadn't told the truth to people in years. Somehow, I think she infected me with her honesty." Smiling wryly, she said, "She was my friend and I've ruined that now. I'm sorry for it."

"You've ruined a hell of a lot more than that."

"No. More truth for you, Cooper. The ruin between

you and Terri, you've done yourself. She's not like us, Cooper," Celeste said. "She's real. When she offers her heart, it has no strings. No expectation for reward. It simply *is*."

Cooper scrubbed both hands across his face. She was right and he knew it. Hell, he'd known it all along. Terri was different. Terri said what she thought and didn't have a dishonest bone in her body. And he hadn't trusted her. Because he'd lived for so long looking cynically at everything, he hadn't recognized *honest* when it finally showed up.

Damn it. He'd let her get away. He'd had something real. Something most people never found and he'd let it go.

"I'm leaving," Celeste said. "If you see Terri again—"

"If?"

"—please tell her I'm sorry for hurting her."

"What do you mean *if* I see her?" Cooper demanded.

"Didn't I tell you? She left."

Panic nearly blinded him. "Left? Left for where?"

"She said to St. George, in Utah somewhere. Her mother's house." Celeste swung her black leather bag across her shoulder, opened the door, then stopped. "She loves you, you know."

"How do you know?" Cooper's gaze snapped to hers. "Did she tell you that?"

"Yes."

"Well, she didn't tell *me*!" And why the hell not? In the midst of that fight they'd had, why hadn't she thrown those words at him? Looking for sympathy or

an edge into wheedling him around to her way of thinking and—that was exactly why she hadn't told him.

Terri didn't play games.

Celeste shook her head at him and asked sadly, "Can
you blame her? Don't be foolish, Cooper. Go after her.
I once walked away from you. I don't recommend it."

"Who does this?" Terri demanded as they barreled
down the highway toward St. George in her brand-new,
shiny red convertible.

Jan stroked the leather dashboard as she would a
lover. "Who cares? He bought you a car before he
turned into Jerk Of The Year. Call it a win and let it
go."

"It's not that easy." Of course Cooper would do
something like this. When she'd joined Jan at the valet
stand, the car was waiting for her.

"That's not my car," she'd said.

"Yes, ma'am, it is," the valet said. "Mr. Hayes
bought it for you a week ago. Said you needed to drive
something decent."

When her eyes fired, the young valet backed up fast
and hid in the valet booth. She couldn't blame him.
Naturally, Jan was thrilled with the new car and had
hopped right in.

Terri, though, turned and shot a hard look at the top
of the hotel as if she could glare at Cooper from there.
He just tossed her car aside and got her a new one without bothering to tell her? What kind of person did that?

Cooper had bought this car for her a week ago,
back when he was supposedly still softening her up

to get rid of her. Why would he do it? And why hadn't he said anything to her about the car, just waiting to let her discover it on her own? Why wouldn't he have told her?

But even as she mentally did gymnastics trying to convince herself that Cooper wasn't really the bastard Jan had named him, Terri remembered Celeste. In his suite. Wearing a towel. About to join said bastard in the shower.

Nothing could have been clearer than that, right? The sting of tears hit her eyes again and she was grateful for the sunglasses she wore. Terri didn't want Jan to see her cry over him. Heck, she didn't want to see *herself* cry any more tears over Cooper. She'd cried a river and it hadn't helped. Hadn't changed a thing.

"Come on, Terri, admit it." Jan shouted to be heard over the roar of the wind. "Your car was on its last legs—wheels. It wasn't going to last another winter."

"It didn't have to make it through snow. It lived in Las Vegas now."

"And now you have a Vegas car." Shaking her head and throwing her arms high to feel the wind rushing at them, Jan said, "A shiny, showgirl car! Red convertible, girl! Look on the bright side. You have this great car that had to cost him a fortune. *And*, you're not going anywhere, so you're going to totally ruin his day. Every day."

Slowly, Terri smiled and stepped harder on the gas. "You have a point. How fast can we get to Mom's house, do you think?"

Jan grinned. "Let's find out."

* * *

Terri didn't bother to knock. She just walked into the small, lovely house her mother and aunt shared. It was a two-bedroom, two-bath Spanish-style patio home on the golf course. Connie spent most days out on the patio, checking out the retired golfers, looking for her fourth husband.

Terri's mom spent most days laughing at Connie.

"Mom?" She stepped into the entryway, with Jan right behind her. She'd expected to have her mom and aunt running to greet her. And if not that, at least she had thought her *dog* would be glad to see her.

"Seems awfully quiet. Maybe they're not home," Jan said, peeking into the living room as Terri closed the door. "Uh-oh."

"What? What's wrong?" Terri pushed past her and stopped dead when she spotted Cooper, comfortably seated on her mother's couch, the traitorous Daisy stretched out across his lap. "Cooper—"

"Terri, honey!" Her mother rushed in from the kitchen, carrying a wooden tray holding a frosted pitcher of iced tea, three glasses and a plate of cookies. "You made wonderful time. That new car Cooper gave you must be a wonder to drive."

"I. He. What?" Terri shook her head, stared from Cooper to her mother and back again. "How do you know about the car?"

"Well, Cooper told me, of course." Carol Ferguson shook her head, then smoothed her perfect blond hair. "It was a relief to me, I'll admit it. Your poor old car was running on prayers."

"A relief," Cooper repeated softly.

Terri glared at him.

"You should have seen his arrival," her mother said, practically glowing as she looked at Cooper. "Do you know, his helicopter landed right on the golf course? People will be talking about it for months!"

"Helicopter?"

He shrugged and continued petting Daisy. "My pilot put down quickly, then took off again. I don't think it did any harm to the course itself."

"Oh, I'm sure it didn't," Carol said. "It was so exciting."

"I bet," Terri said.

"Your mom's been very nice, letting me stay to wait for you," Cooper said, his long, clever fingers rubbing Daisy's belly until the dog was a quivering bowl of jelly.

"Your dog's a traitor," Jan whispered and walked over to give Terri's mom a big hug.

"So good to see you, sweetheart," Mom said. "I love your hair."

Jan grinned, then shifted a hard-eyed look on Cooper. "I'm glad to see you, too, Mom. But I sort of question your taste in guests."

"Now, Jan…"

"Nice to meet you, too," Cooper said wryly.

"Why don't I just go and get a few more glasses for the tea," Carol said, taking Jan's arm and dragging her off, too. She called back over her shoulder, "Connie's assaulting one of the golfers but she should be along soon…"

In the quiet of the living room, Terri felt completely off balance. In a million years, she never would have expected to find Cooper here. With her mom. And her dog. All comfy and cozy.

The living room was bright and cheerful, with a vase of fall flowers in the center of the coffee table. The furniture was plain but good quality and thanks to her mother, the room was tidy, tables polished, the scent of the flowers flavoring the air. The blinds were open, allowing the fall sun to slant into the room and paint gold stripes on the floor.

And while she stalled, looking at a room that she knew as well as her own home, Cooper watched her. She couldn't tell what he was thinking and she wished she could. But she knew very well what she was *feeling,* so she went with that.

"Why are you here?"

"Because you are."

"Cooper—"

"I needed to talk to you, Terri," he said, "and you'd already left the hotel."

She shot a dirty look at Daisy who was now doing the dog version of a purr. "I suppose I should thank you for the car."

"But you don't want to."

"No, I don't." She shifted her glare to him. "You got rid of my car without so much as asking me."

"Your car was a disgrace to all cars everywhere."

She took a breath. Hard to argue that point, but she tried. "It wasn't any of your business."

"You're welcome."

Daisy sighed and opened one eye to look at Terri as if to say, *Don't ruin this for me.*

"I like your dog."

"She's apparently a shameless tramp with very low standards in men."

He winced at that barb. "I also like your mom and her sister. Though your mom warned me to watch out for your aunt Connie."

Terri brushed that aside. Why were they talking about this? About things that didn't matter. "You're not Connie's type. She likes them rich and old enough to not last long."

He laughed shortly and the sound tore at her. How could he be acting like nothing was wrong?

"I'm so sorry you had to cut your shower with Celeste short," she said. "That must have been painful for both of you."

He scowled at her. "I know what she told you. Damn it. I wasn't even there when you stopped by my room. Celeste set the whole thing up to get me back, to chase you off."

Terri swayed from the impact of his words. She'd liked Celeste. And somehow the fact that she had lied to Terri was almost worse than the thought that she'd been showering with Cooper. Almost. "Seems there was a lot of that going on. Dave, Celeste, *you*, all working overtime to get rid of me."

"Seems like it worked, too." Cooper gave Daisy one last stroke, then set her aside and stood up. Shoving both hands into the pockets of his slacks, he said, "Celeste told me you left. That you came here."

"It *didn't* work," Terri countered, taking a step farther into the room. "I'm not leaving Las Vegas, Cooper. I only came here to get my dog. Then I'm going back to the StarFire. You can't force me out. I won't go."

"Good."

"Just because you think— What?"

"I said good." He walked closer in a few long, determined strides. "I don't want you to go."

"Well, that's news to me," she said, because she couldn't believe him. Not anymore. "You told me just last night that the plan had always been to get rid of me. To buy me out."

"Yeah, it was." He yanked one hand free, rubbed the back of his neck, then pinned her with an ice-blue gaze she couldn't look away from. "Hell, Jacob sprung you on me. I didn't even know you existed and suddenly I acquired a partner. One who didn't know anything about the business. I was pissed. But then, things changed."

"Really? Last night you accused me of backstabbing you."

"Yeah, see, this is why I had to talk to you. I was wrong."

Terri blinked at him and shook her head as if she hadn't heard him right. "Well, there's something I never thought I'd hear from you."

"If you need me to say it again, I will," Cooper ground out. "I won't enjoy it, but I'll do it." He came closer and Terri stood her ground, not giving an inch. "Dave told me everything. How he was working against me all these years. How he used you. How even if his

plan with you had failed, he was prepared to sell me out once he got what he thought he deserved. And I never saw it in him.

"But even if he hadn't confessed, I never should have thought it was you. It's just not your style, Terri. You're so damn honest it's a shock to most people. Apparently, even to me."

She heard the pain in his voice and her instinct was to soothe. To offer comfort. But she didn't. Because he'd hurt *her*. But that sounded so damn petty, she had to say, "I'm sorry about your friend."

"You really are, aren't you?" Shaking his head, he reached for her but she moved away. His hands fell to his sides. "Even after everything he did. Everything I did. I was a complete ass last night."

"No argument here."

A wry smile curved his mouth briefly. "I didn't expect one. But I am so damn sorry. I've spent so many years dealing with people who always have an agenda, I forgot what it was like to be around someone who didn't."

"As apologies go, that was pretty good," she admitted. Her heart hurt, just looking at him. Everything in her wanted to go into his arms and feel him hold her. But she didn't, because they still had more to say.

"I'm just getting started," he said and this time when he reached out to cup her shoulders, she didn't slide out of his grasp. "You're the best thing that ever happened to me and I don't want to lose you. I want to start each day looking into your eyes. I want to hold you while

we fall asleep together. You're everything I need, Terri. That's why I'm here."

"I thought you came to talk to me."

"Well, yeah, and to ask you to marry me."

"Marry you?"

He grinned. "Yes. I want us to be together. Always. A team. Terri, we're great together and I want it to be permanent. A commitment. From each of us."

Terri didn't even know how to react.

"We can build a house because I know you want kids and so do I and maybe a hotel isn't the best place to raise them—"

"Kids?" Her heart picked up speed and her breath got short and fast.

"Yes, a family. " He pulled her in close enough that she had to tip her head back to look into ice-blue eyes that were suddenly as warm as a summer lake. "You love me," he said. "Celeste told me."

"Celeste had a lot to say," Terri muttered.

"And I love you," Cooper said softly.

"You do?" she whispered.

"Of course I do. Why do you think I'm here? Why do you think I bought you that car so you wouldn't end up broken down on the side of the road in the middle of the desert? I loved you even then. I just didn't want to."

"And now you do."

"Now I have no choice," he muttered. "I want you. I need you. I love you. One night without you and I was going nuts. I kept reaching for you during the night and you weren't there. Damned if I'll spend another night like last night."

"I missed you, too," she said. "But after last night, I thought it was over."

"It's never going to be over for us, Terri," he said, his gaze moving over her features like a gentle touch. "We're supposed to be together. I get that now. And we'll build the damn house wherever you want it—"

"No."

"No? What do you mean *no*?" His brow furrowed, he stared at her through narrowed eyes.

"I mean, we'll live at the hotel. My suite is huge, so I'm sure yours is big enough for a family..."

"Six thousand square feet," he told her. "Five bedrooms, six bathrooms."

"Oh, my God." She laughed up at him. "Yeah, that's big enough. And we have the roof garden—we can make the Plexiglas higher..."

"If that's what you want, sure."

"And Jan's going to be living in my suite so—"

His eyebrows went high on his forehead. "You mean your friend who hates me?"

Terri grinned. "I hired her as my executive assistant."

He grinned back at her. "Of course you did. And you'll probably have better luck with your best friend than I had with mine."

"I'm sorry about Dave."

"Yeah," he said. "Me, too. Well, if we're going to be neighbors, I'll buy Jan a car so she'll like me."

"No, you won't—"

"I like red, too," Jan called from the kitchen.

"Perfect." Terri laughed and leaned her forehead against his chest.

"See?" Cooper grinned and he looked so wildly happy that Terri's heart fluttered. "She likes me already. So does your mom. And your aunt. And you love me, Terri. Tell me you love me."

She looked up at him. "I love you. And yes, I'll marry you."

"Damn straight." He kissed her hard and fast, then let her go long enough to dig into his pocket for a small, black velvet jewelry box. He flipped the lid open and Terri gasped. "It's a star sapphire. Like the StarFire. And the diamonds around it are just for show."

Shaken, she held her left hand out and he slid the ring onto her finger. The stone was huge, with a blast of color at the heart of it, looking just like a star. The setting was gorgeous and it fit as if made for her. "It's a beautiful show."

"Are you sure you want to live at the hotel?" he asked. "What about your fear of heights?"

Sighing, she said, "As it turns out, the only thing I'm afraid of is losing you."

His thumbs smoothed over her cheeks. "Never gonna happen. You and I are a hell of a team, Terri. And that's how it's going to stay."

"I do love you so much, Cooper."

"I'll never get tired of hearing it."

"Can we come out now?" Carol Ferguson called. "We'd love to see the ring!"

"In a minute," Cooper shouted, then whispered to only Terri. "First things first."

Get 4 FREE REWARDS!

We'll send you 2 FREE Books plus 2 FREE Mystery Gifts.

Harlequin® **Desire** books feature heroes who have it all: wealth, status, incredible good looks... everything but the right woman.

FREE Value Over **$20**

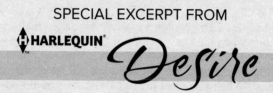
She was going to be interviewing Isaiah's potential wife.

The man she had been in love with since she was a
teenage idiot, and was still in love with now that she was
an idiot in her late twenties.

There were a whole host of reasons she'd never, ever
let on about her feelings for him.

She loved her job. She loved Isaiah's family, who were
the closest thing she had to a family of her own.

She was also living in the small town of Copper Ridge,
Oregon, which was a bit strange for a girl from Seattle,
but she did like it. It had a different pace. But that meant
there was less opportunity for a social life. There were
fewer people to interact with. By default she, and the
other folks in town, ended up spending a lot of their free
time with the people they worked with every day. There
was nothing wrong with that. But it was just…

Mostly there wasn't enough of a break from Isaiah on
any given day.

But then, she also didn't enforce one. Didn't take one. She supposed she couldn't really blame the small-town location when the likely culprit of the entire situation was her.

"Place whatever ad you need to," he said, his tone abrupt. "When you meet the right woman, you'll know."

"I'll know," she echoed lamely.

"Yes. Nobody knows me better than you do, Poppy. I have faith that you'll pick the right wife for me."

With those awful words still ringing in the room, Isaiah left her there, sitting at her desk, feeling numb.

The fact of the matter was, she probably could pick him a perfect wife. Someone who would facilitate his life, and give him space when he needed it. Someone who was beautiful and fabulous in bed.

Yes, she knew exactly what Isaiah Grayson would think made a woman the perfect wife for him.

The sad thing was, Poppy didn't possess very many of those qualities herself.

And what she so desperately wanted was for Isaiah's perfect wife to be her.

But dreams were for other women. They always had been. Which meant some other woman was going to end up with Poppy's dream.

While she played matchmaker to the whole affair.

Don't miss what happens when Isaiah decides it's Poppy *who should be his convenient wife in*
Want Me, Cowboy *by USA TODAY bestselling author Maisey Yates, part of her Copper Ridge series!*

Available November 2018 wherever
Harlequin® Desire books and ebooks are sold.

www.Harlequin.com

Want to give in to temptation with
steamy tales of irresistible desire?

Check out **Harlequin® Presents®,
Harlequin® Desire** and
Harlequin® Kimani™ Romance books!

New books available every month!

CONNECT WITH US AT:

Facebook.com/groups/HarlequinConnection

 Facebook.com/HarlequinBooks

 Twitter.com/HarlequinBooks

 Instagram.com/HarlequinBooks

Pinterest.com/HarlequinBooks

ReaderService.com

**ROMANCE WHEN
YOU NEED IT**

PGENRE2018

Love Harlequin romance?

DISCOVER.

Be the first to find out about promotions, news and exclusive content!

 Facebook.com/HarlequinBooks

Twitter.com/HarlequinBooks

 Instagram.com/HarlequinBooks

 Pinterest.com/HarlequinBooks

ReaderService.com

EXPLORE.

Sign up for the Harlequin e-newsletter and download a free book from any series at **TryHarlequin.com.**

CONNECT.

Join our Harlequin community to share your thoughts and connect with other romance readers!
Facebook.com/groups/HarlequinConnection

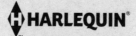 HARLEQUIN®

**ROMANCE WHEN
YOU NEED IT**

HSOCIAL2018